THE WOMBLES TO THE RESCUE

THE WOMBLES TO THE RESCUE

Elisabeth Beresford

Illustrated by Nick Price

First published in Great Britain in 1974
by Ernest Benn Limited
This Large Print edition published 2012
by AudioGO Ltd
by arrangement with Bloomsbury Publishing Plc

ISBN: 978 1445 81996 9

British Library Cataloguing in Publication Data available

Printed and bound in Great Britain by
MPG Books Group Limited

For Alderney

PAWS FOR THOUGHT

AN ADDITIONAL NOTE FROM GREAT UNCLE BULGARIA

When I first saw Elisabeth Beresford, I knew that I had met the right Human Being to whom the Womble adventures could be told. It was Boxing Day and she was with her children, Marcus and Kate, walking on Wimbledon Common. They were letting off steam, having had to be on best behaviour over Christmas as their house had been full of elderly relations. I heard Elisabeth's daughter say, 'Oh Ma, it's wonderful on Wombledon Common' and that was it! Elisabeth became aware of our existence, the burrow, and the way we Wombles recycle all the rubbish you Human Beings leave behind.

She told me that she had written lots of children's books, including magic stories, so I told her all about us but I made her promise never to give away the location of the burrow. Since then, we've appeared in books, made records and appeared on television. The young Wombles think it's great fun but I prefer a quiet life. *Tsk, tsk.*

I am very happy to give my pawprint to this reprint (Bungo insisted I use that joke) and hope you enjoy our adventures as much as we did.

Now I must go because Orinoco has just found today's edition of *The Times*. Of course, he has gone straight to the kitchen to claim his reward from Madame Cholet. I think I heard him muttering something about daisy and dandelion fizz . . .

Carry on Wombling.

Great Uncle Bulgaria
The Womble Burrow
Wimbledon Common

CHAPTER 1

GREAT UNCLE BULGARIA GETS A LETTER

'It's certainly very nice to be back,' said Great Uncle Bulgaria, looking round Wimbledon Common.

The sun was just coming up, and there were long shadows across the grass, which was sparkling with dew. Over towards the Windmill, a small round figure was trotting along with a tidy-bag in one paw and a pointed stick (which had once been an umbrella shaft) in the other.

'One of my Wombles out working already,' said Great Uncle Bulgaria, hitching his shawl more closely round his shoulders, as there was a decidedly cool nip in the air. 'How very gratifying . . .'

'Yes, I dare say,' said Tobermory, who was standing by the Wombles' own home-made car, the Silver Womble, which was still packed tight with

1

sleepy-eyed young Wombles, who were all starting to yawn rather noisily behind their paws. 'I dare say you're quite right, Bulgaria, you usually are; but, be that as it may, it's high time we all got safely home inside the burrow. Come along, you young Wombles, out you get. Quietly now . . .'

The young Wombles stopped yawning and rubbing their eyes and climbed down out of the car.

'I'll tell you what,' said Bungo, who was as bossy and know-all as ever. 'The burrow looks different to me. The front door's not the same for a start. I'll tell you what . . .'

'No, you won't,' said Tomsk. 'You've been telling us all across London about *everything*. You told us about the traffic lights, and the roads and the bridges. You're ALWAYS telling us and . . .'

'I don't care about all that,' said Orinoco, 'as long as it's breakfast time. I'm ever so hungry, you know. What I'd really fancy would be toadstool scramble on fried moss bread followed by bracken marmalade and dandelion toast with a few fresh hazelnuts for afters and . . .'

'QUIET!' roared Tobermory.

The young Wombles all stopped arguing and whispering and pushing, and even Orinoco stopped rubbing his stomach because, when Tobermory used that tone of voice, it meant that something serious was going to happen.

'This,' said Tobermory, 'is a very important moment in Womble history. We Wombles have left Hyde Park [See *The Wombles at Work.*] to return to Wimbledon Common, because when all's said and done, we ARE the Wombles of Wimbledon. Over to you, Bulgaria.'

2

Great Uncle Bulgaria leant on his stick, and looked over his spectacles at all the young Wombles. He would very much have liked to make a speech, but he could see that everyone was rather tired, so he only said, 'We've been away from our Wimbledon burrow for some time, because, as you all know, we had to leave when the heavy lorries kept roaring round Tibbet's Corner. While there was so much traffic on the road, this burrow just wasn't safe. Now, it *is* perfectly safe. Thanks to information from Advance Womble Scouting Parties we know that heavy traffic has been re-routed. So we're home again, and now that we *are* here, we must all pull together. We must . . . goodness gracious me, what is THAT?'

THAT was a rusty, squeaking, really horrible noise, which made everybody's fur stand on end as the door of the burrow opened. A small, square (even for a Womble) figure appeared in the doorway. He seemed to be quite old as his fur was nearly as white as Great Uncle Bulgaria's and he was wearing a very battered yellow panama hat, and a large apron made of sacking, which came down to his toes. In one paw he was holding a flowerpot, and in the other a bent kitchen fork.

The elderly Womble looked at all the other Wombles with his bright little eyes, and then he touched the brim of his hat with the fork, and nodded at Great Uncle Bulgaria, who for once in his long life didn't seem to know what to say. Then the elderly Womble turned and went hurrying off across the Common, and very soon vanished in the bushes.

'Dear, dear, DEAR me,' said Great Uncle Bulgaria, finding his voice at last, 'that surely can't have been . . . no, no it's impossible . . . but it must have been. Goodness gracious ME!'

'Who?' said Bungo, who was jumping up and down with curiosity.

'Cousin Botany,' said Tobermory. 'Haven't seen him for years. Thought he'd retired. He came to this country from Australia, when he was very young. Came by sailing ship, I seem to recall. You know, Bulgaria, this front door's in a shocking state. The hinges just haven't been properly oiled. *Tsk, tsk, tsk.*'

'Cousin Botany,' said Great Uncle Bulgaria. 'Now why has he suddenly turned up here, I wonder? Not that I've anything against Botany, indeed I'm very fond of him, but he's a—er—rather unusual Womble in his way.'

By this time, everybody, even Orinoco, was so interested in their unusual relation that they had all bunched together in a group, quite forgetting how sleepy they were.

'Why is he unusual?' asked Wellington in a whisper.

'Because he doesn't like talking, that's why,' said Tobermory briskly. 'Unlike some I could mention,' and he looked hard at Bungo, who tried to pretend that he was busy smoothing down his fur. 'Which reminds me, Bulgaria, the sun's well up now, and that means there'll be some Human Beings coming on to the Common soon. You know how noisy they are, so perhaps we'd better get nice and snug inside the burrow, eh?'

Great Uncle Bulgaria, who appeared to have gone off into a dream about something or another, nodded and led the way indoors, shaking his white head as he did so. Everybody else followed on

4

behind him, and Tobermory, after looking at the rust on the front door hinges yet again while going '*tsk, tsk, tsk*' under his breath, returned to the Silver Womble which was now empty. He drove it round to the back of the burrow where he discovered, as he had known all along that he would do, that the hinges were in a bad state on the garage door as well.

The Silver Womble slid into its old familiar home and stopped. It is totally Tobermory's invention and it is the only car of its kind in the world. He had recently adapted it to run entirely on clockwork, so it is silent, smell-less and costs nothing to use. Tobermory climbed out and took a large duster from his apron pocket, and dusted the windscreen and then the bonnet and finally all the bumpers. As WOM I was not particularly dusty, let alone dirty, this was a certain, sure sign that Tobermory was rather worried about something.

'I'll tell you what,' said Tobermory to WOM I, as he put away his duster, and sighed deeply, 'and I know I sound just like Bungo, but I'm worried. Things aren't as they should be. It's something to do with us Wombles, and something to do with the burrow—which doesn't feel *right* somehow—and something to do with finding old Cousin Botany here! Now, why should he come out of his retirement, eh? When a Womble gets to his age, he has a *right* to take things easy. Why, dear me, he must be . . . one hundred, one hundred and fifty . . . Hallo . . . what's that?'

It was the distant sound of a bell being rung very importantly. It was a particular sort of a bell and, as Tobermory had made it in the first place out of old tin cans and bits of this and pieces of that, he

5

recognised it at once. He stopped feeling a little bit afraid and a tiny bit worried because, like every other Womble in the world, he knew very well that when a bell was sounded in that *particular* way it could only mean one thing.

'Breakfast time,' said Tobermory and sniffed deeply. 'And what's more I do believe it's toadstool scramble on fried moss bread . . . Quite my most favourite food really . . .'

Of course all the other Wombles of Wimbledon were saying exactly the same thing and their bright little eyes were all turned towards the kitchen where Madame Cholet (the best Womble cook, probably, that there's ever been) had been working away from the moment she had returned to the Wimbledon burrow.

'*Tiens*,' said Madame Cholet who, because of her name, likes to talk in French from time to time, '*tiens*, come along and start eating or everything will be ruined!'

Nobody needed to be told twice and for quite a long time there was no sound at all except for busy eating noises. It wasn't until Orinoco had chewed his way through SIX slices of dandelion toast that Great Uncle Bulgaria got to his back paws and, having banged on the table for silence, said, 'Welcome back to the Wimbledon burrow, Wombles.'

'Hear, hear,' said Wellington.

'Hear, hear, hear,' said Bungo, who never likes to be outdone.

'Mmmmmm,' said Tomsk, who was wondering in a vague sort of way if he'd be able to go swimming in Queen's Mere quite soon.

'*Zzzzzz*,' said Orinoco, who was just drifting off

into a nice forty winks.

'Welcome back,' repeated Great Uncle Bulgaria, getting out his second pair of spectacles and putting them on his nose so that he could look over and through them in a rather scary way, which made even Bungo stop whispering. 'But, although it is very pleasant to be back in our old home burrow, I do feel that we should all realise that . . . oh dear me, what is it now?'

Great Uncle Bulgaria, Tobermory, Madame Cholet and everybody else turned to look towards the door, which had just opened rather noisily, because its hinges were somewhat rusty.

A small square figure wearing a battered panama hat, a long sacking apron, and a rather puzzled expression appeared in the opening.

'Cousin Botany,' said Great Uncle Bulgaria just a little bit crossly, 'we're all very glad that you've come to pay us a visit, but is there anything in particular that you would like to say to us?'

Cousin Botany scratched behind his ear with his kitchen fork, looked under the brim of his hat, wrinkled his nose and then very slowly shook his head in such a sad sort of way that all the young Wombles felt quite scared.

'Have something to eat,' said Madame Cholet. 'A slice of dandelion toast, yes?'

'Thank you kindly, no,' replied Cousin Botany in a slow, deep voice. 'Had my meal at sunup. This is for you, Bulgaria. Came while you were away over the other side of the river. I'd have brought it to you, except I had work to do.'

And Cousin Botany took a rather crumpled, muddy envelope out of his apron pocket, dusted it with the back of his paw, and gave it to Great

Uncle Bulgaria. Before anybody else could say a word Cousin Botany had hurried out of the room. A few seconds later they heard the awful screeching sound of the front door being opened and then shut.

'He always was rather a *strange* sort of Womble, even when he was young,' Great Uncle Bulgaria said behind his paw to Tobermory. But Tobermory only nodded and grunted under his breath, because he was busy writing out a long list of odd jobs that he had already noticed needed doing round the burrow. It started with 'No. 1. Oil hinges', and he had already got to No. 7., which was 'Water pipes leaking!'

'There's a lot to be done,' said Tobermory, putting his pencil behind his ear. 'I can't understand it really, because I gave *exact* instructions as to what needed repairing and decorating and looking after in the burrow while we were away and . . . Bulgaria, are you listening?'

'Not very much,' said Great Uncle Bulgaria, 'as

8

I have other things on my mind at the moment. Very well, young Wombles, take your plates and knives and forks out to the kitchen and stack them neatly. Breakfast is over. No, Orinoco, it is no use looking at me like that. If you have *one more* slice of toast you will be *sick*. You can all do the washing-up later. Off you go to bed and have a good day's sleep.'

The young Wombles did as they were told, except for Bungo. He kept telling everybody else what to do, until, in a fur-prickling way, he felt Great Uncle Bulgaria looking at him, so that even he kept quiet until he was climbing up into his own nice familiar bunk, and then he couldn't help saying, 'I'll tell you what . . .'

'Zzzzz,' said Orinoco, who slept in the bunk down below, and who was already hauling a nice cosy blanket up to his chin, while he wondered what Madame Cholet was going to cook for supper.

'What?' said Tomsk, who was doing his exercises further along the dormitory. 'One, two and touch your back paws, one, two and stretch up from the floors . . .'

'That's not proper English,' said Wellington, who was putting all his books in order on the shelf above his bed. 'There's only one floor in here, you know. You'd have to do your exercises all over the burrow if you want to say "floors". Sorry to mention it.'

'That's all right,' said Tomsk, 'only I say floors, because then I remember how to do my exercises. It helps if it's poetry. What, Bungo?'

'Oh, don't mind me,' said Bungo, 'don't take any notice of ME, I'm not important I know that . . .'

9

And he hung right over the edge of his bunk and looked down at Orinoco, who really was asleep by now, and dreaming of scrambled bracken pie. 'All I want to say IS, what's Cousin Botany doing in this burrow and *why* is he here and *what* exactly is going on and . . .'

'Lights out,' said Madame Cholet, appearing in the doorway. 'Sleep well, my little ones, and no more talking!'

'Ooooooh, drat!' said Bungo, but he did as he was told.

Strangely enough, further along the burrow in his study, Great Uncle Bulgaria, who was just reading the crumpled, dusty letter which Cousin Botany had given him for at least the tenth time, now said almost exactly the same thing.

'Oooooh, drat! I suppose I shall have to go. What do you think, Tobermory? Tobermory, are you there?'

' 'Course I'm here,' growled Tobermory, who was getting crosser by the minute, and he crawled out from underneath Great Uncle Bulgaria's bookcase and scribbled in his notebook 'No. 22. Woodworm in b-cases (bad)'.

'It's this letter,' said Great Uncle Bulgaria. 'It's from the Wombles in the United States of America. They want me to go over there as soon as possible.'

'Well, you can't,' said Tobermory, sitting down in the rocking chair, and taking the weight off his back paws. 'You're needed here in Wimbledon, Bulgaria. Things are in a shocking state in this burrow. Shocking.'

'I dare say,' said Great Uncle Bulgaria, 'but this letter is marked Womble-Urgent and you know

10

what THAT means . . .'

There was a long, long pause during which the two wise old Wombles looked at each other. Then Tobermory took off his bowler hat, wiped his handkerchief round the inside, put the handkerchief away and replaced the hat on his grey head.

'Like that, is it?' said Tobermory. 'Well, you'll have to go then, Bulgaria. *Tsk, tsk, tsk*. I don't know what the Womble world's coming to, really I don't!'

'Neither do I,' agreed Great Uncle Bulgaria, 'but one thing I *am* sure about is, those rockers need oiling! Put them on your list, there's a good Womble.'

CHAPTER 2

TOBERMORY SEES TROUBLE AHEAD

All the young Wombles were far too excited about being back in their old home burrow to notice that Great Uncle Bulgaria, Tobermory and Madame Cholet were rather quiet and thoughtful. After all, it's not every day that you swap burrows and so get the chance to explore all your old, familiar, favourite places.

'I'll tell you what,' said Bungo. 'I'd forgotten how many ups and downs there are here. Hyde Park was a bit on the flat side.'

'It was smashing for swimming in though,' said Tomsk, and then he added hastily as he saw Bungo's mouth open, 'I mean the *Serpentine* was smashing for swimming in. Bigger.'

'But full of boats and people a lot of the time. Human Beings don't do any of that sort of thing in Queen's Mere,' said Bungo, who was in that mood when he wasn't going to have anybody say anything against Wimbledon Common, because he was so happy about being back there again.

'Mmmm,' said Tomsk, and he went stumping off with his front paws clasped behind his back and his chin on his chest.

'Gone to look for golf balls, I expect,' said Wellington. 'He misses Omsk, you know.'

'Dull sort of Womble *he* was,' said Bungo. 'Hardly spoke really. I wonder if all the Russian Wombles are like that?'

As Omsk was the only Russian Womble anybody had met and had, only quite by chance, come into contact with his British Womble relations, nobody could answer this question.

'I don't know,' said Wellington, 'but Omsk and Tomsk got on very well together, so now Tomsk misses Omsk. It's funny really, leaving a Russian Womble behind in the Hyde Park burrow to look after it.'

'There's nothing much left to *look* after,' said Bungo, 'now that Human Beings have suddenly started being so tidy. They don't leave rubbish and stuff lying about like they used to. Why, I remember when I was quite a young Womble . . .'

'You still are,' said Orinoco, who had been shifting round and about to make himself a nice cosy bed in the bracken, as he very much wanted to have a little nap in order to get his strength up for tea. 'You still *are* a young Womble, because I can remember when you chose your name out of Great Uncle Bulgaria's atlas, and it wasn't very long ago either. Even then you were far too bossy, and now you're bossier than ever. You think you know everything, but you jolly well DON'T, SO SHUT UP for a bit and go AWAY.'

13

Bungo was so surprised at this most unexpected attack that he did exactly as he was told (for once) and Wellington, who had been almost equally surprised, said, 'That was a bit hard, Orinoco, wasn't it?'

'Umph,' replied Orinoco, pulling the brim of his hat down over his eyes, 'p'raps. But I'll tell you one thing, I just can't *stand* bossy Wombles. Now DO be quiet!'

'If that's not being bossy, I don't know what is,' muttered Wellington. 'What's the matter with you all of a sudden? It makes me feel all itchy and scratchy under my fur when Wombles start snapping at each other . . .'

'Zzzzzzz,' said Orinoco.

Wellington heaved one of his enormous sighs which made his large, round spectacles slide right down his nose, and then he went off after Bungo, who was sulking near the Windmill.

'I thought it was going to be lovely being back here on Wimbledon Common,' said Bungo, 'but it's not all lovely after all. In fact, it's quite nasty in some ways. Orinoco's cross, Tomsk won't talk and the burrow's not half as comfortable as it used to be, because nothing seems to be working properly. And I'll tell you what, I think it's got something to do with Cousin Botany. So there!'

It was an unkind thing to say, and Bungo, although very bossy-and-know-it-all, was not nasty about other Wombles, which just goes to show how itchy and scratchy *he* was starting to feel too. Wellington didn't know what to reply, but fortunately Tomsk came bounding up at this point with his paws full of golf balls.

'Come on,' he said. 'It's no good standing

14

around with faces as long as today and tomorrow AND the day after that. Remember the old Womble saying, *Some golf every day keeps the crossness away.* Come on.'

So for the next few hours matters weren't too bad overground on the Common. Orinoco was snoozing his temper away, Tomsk was playing hole after hole in three strokes, Wellington (who was hopeless at all games) was hitting the ball sideways, upwards and backwards (but never forwards) so he had to keep scurrying off in all directions to retrieve it, while Bungo leant heavily on the golf club which Tomsk had given him, and told the other two Wombles exactly what they *should* be doing. He was so busy talking he didn't have time to actually play any golf himself.

Great Uncle Bulgaria came out of the burrow with Tobermory and went for a little stroll, during which they watched the young Wombles, and Great Uncle Bulgaria said, 'They're overtired and overexcited, because of the move back here, and they are also a bit bored because now we *have* moved, there isn't so much to do. Tobermory, we have to face the fact that now Human Beings are being just a little more careful about NOT dropping litter all over the place, there isn't much tidying up for our young working Wombles.'

'It's all right for some,' said Tobermory. 'I've got more work to do than I can manage. The burrow's in a shocking state, Bulgaria. Shocking. And I left such careful instructions as to main-tain-ance too. I just don't understand it. Wombles aren't what they were when *I* was young.'

'Ho-hum,' said Great Uncle Bulgaria, putting up a paw to hide a small smile, 'nothing ever *is* the

15

same as it used to be. Not even Human Beings. But the reason for all the trouble in the burrow has nothing to do with us Wombles. It's because Human Beings keep running short of things. They haven't got enough paper and cardboard, there isn't enough plastic this and that to go round, they've got what they call "an energy crisis" . . .'

'Lazy lot. I'd give 'em energy what-name,' growled Tobermory. 'If people worked as hard as we Wombles do, there wouldn't be all this silly nonsense. I tell you, Bulgaria . . .'

And Tobermory did at great length, for like all the others, he was feeling thoroughly out of sorts and Great Uncle Bulgaria listened patiently and said, 'Oh yes' and 'I see' and 'Ho-hum' from time to time, because he knew very well that you can't hurry a Womble who has got a grievance to get off his chest. Finally Tobermory stopped talking and just stood there with his nose turned down at the tip and his grey moustache drooping.

'Yes, yes, yes, I dare say,' murmured Great Uncle Bulgaria, 'but the truth of the matter is, Tobermory, and we must face up to it, that there just isn't enough this, that and the other to go round. Don't let's fuss about whose fault it is, because that does no good at all. Our problems are first, that because at long last Human Beings have started becoming less wasteful, we Wombles haven't got so much to do in the tidying-up line, and secondly that, like Human Beings, we Wombles are also going to find it very difficult to make ends meet.'

'I'm not with you,' muttered Tobermory, staring across the Common in a very grumpy way.

'Why is the front door of the burrow making

16

that dreadful noise every time it's opened?' asked Great Uncle Bulgaria.

'Hinges need oiling.'

'Why haven't they been oiled when you left such careful instructions?'

'No oil.'

'Why are the bookshelves full of holes and rot?'

'No Womble anti-hole-and-rot mixture left in the Workshop.'

'Ho-hum. What stores are left in the pantry?'

'Not many bottles of dried toadstool, bracken flour is low and the powdered dandelion casks are nearly empty. Here, I say, Bulgaria . . .' Tobermory suddenly stopped looking mournful and straightened up, 'you don't mean that WE'RE going to be short of all kinds of useful things AND food?'

'I shouldn't be surprised, Tobermory. It certainly looks like it. It's Womble-world-wide this problem, which is why I've been invited to the United States of America. There's to be this big meeting there to try and work out what's to be done. If we Wombles don't start doing something, goodness knows what might happen.'

'You mustn't go on your own,' said Tobermory, quite forgetting his own troubles, as he looked at his old friend. Nobody knew quite what Great Uncle Bulgaria's age was, but at this particular moment he looked so old and sad that Tobermory felt very worried. 'I'd better come with you,' he said gruffly. 'No good tiring yourself out. I know what these American Wombles are like, all talk-talk-talk . . .'

Tobermory had always been just a little bit jealous of Cousin Yellowstone Womble from

America, and he was quite sure that if some Womble didn't cross the Atlantic with Great Uncle Bulgaria, something simply awful might happen. Great Uncle Bulgaria might become so overworked, he might even fall ill . . .

A great shiver went through Tobermory's grey fur at the very idea and Great Uncle Bulgaria, pulling his MacWomble tartan shawl more closely round his shoulders, said, 'Now then, Tobermory, stop imagining this, that and the other. I agree with you that the American Wombles are great talkers, which is why I've decided to take a great *British* talker with me! And it won't be you, because you've got more than enough work here to get on with. Goodness gracious me, Tobermory, this whole burrow would collapse and vanish if you weren't here to look after it.'

'There's Botany,' said Tobermory, a shade of doubt in his voice. 'He could run the place, I suppose.' He was secretly very pleased about what Great Uncle Bulgaria had just said, but he wasn't going to let on.

'Botany lives in a world of his own. Always has done. That's how he arrived in this country from Australia in the first place so the story goes. He went down to the Sydney docks to look for supplies, climbed on board the first ship he came to, saw something which took his interest and went to investigate it. The next thing he knew was that the ship was heading out to sea with him on board and . . .'

'What *was* it that interested Botany so much?' asked Tobermory, quite forgetting his own worries, as this extraordinary piece of Womble history came to light.

18

'Nobody has ever quite liked to ask,' said Great Uncle Bulgaria rather sternly. 'And Botany has never actually told anybody. He may have forgotten what it was himself. He's a most absent-minded Womble, even more so than Wellington. Which, Tobermory, brings me back to the problem in hand. Botany definitely will NOT do to run this burrow while I'm away. You are the only Womble I can be certain will do the job efficiently. All the other Wombles trust you AND you will know the best way to get everything working properly again.'

'Yes, I dare say,' said Tobermory, 'that's all very fine, Bulgaria. But how, may I ask, *can* I, when I haven't got the STUFF TO DO IT WITH!'

'I'm sure you'll find a way, Tobermory, you always do. Dear me, it's turning quite chilly, I think I shall return to the burrow.'

'Yes, yes, yes, but hang on a moment, Bulgaria. Who *are* you going to take with you on this dratted American trip?'

'I shall announce the name after our meal. I may even make a little speech about the difficult days which lie ahead and the perils which we face in these dark times and . . .'

Great Uncle Bulgaria's voice died away as he marched into the burrow still talking busily. Tobermory took off his bowler hat, wiped his handkerchief round the inside and then sighed rather heavily in very much the same way as Wellington had done earlier.

In the far distance he could see Cousin Botany standing as still as a statue while he stared straight at the ground. In the middle distance Bungo and Tomsk were having a nose to nose argument which Wellington was apparently trying to stop, while

19

nearer at hand still there was an even more familiar sight—Orinoco fast asleep in a bed of bracken. But then, as if he were aware of being looked at, Orinoco stirred, rubbed his paws in his eyes, swung his fat little body out of the bracken and shuffled over to Tobermory.

'Isn't it about mealtime?' asked Orinoco. 'I'm ever so hungry. Moving makes you hungry, you know.'

'Everything makes you hungry,' said Tobermory, 'and yes it is. Off you go, young Womble.' And Tobermory put his bowler hat back on his head, shook his head, blew the whistle he kept in his apron pocket to tell all the other Wombles that it was mealtime, and then said under his breath, 'Here we go again. I can always tell. When my fur prickles in a certain way, that's an OMEN. There's Bulgaria off travelling, the burrow in a shocking state, and this energy whatsits name. In fact, here we go AGAIN!'

He was quite right.

CHAPTER 3

WELLINGTON VANISHES

As Great Uncle Bulgaria always enjoyed making speeches, Tobermory was rather worried that the old Womble might go on and on and ON talking. However, luckily for everyone (except perhaps Great Uncle Bulgaria), all the Wombles were so tired that after the first few words they began nodding off, their heads getting heavier and heavier until their chins came to rest on their chests. As the Wombles are the politest creatures in the world they did try to keep awake, but it was no good and first one and then another started to snore until the noise rose and fell like the sound of a distant sea.

'. . . and furthermore in these difficult times,' went on Great Uncle Bulgaria, turning over a page in his notes and then there was a simply tremendous . . . 'zzzzzzzzzZZZZZ' . . . right in the front row as Orinoco was having a nice noisy forty winks there, and Great Uncle Bulgaria looked up from his notes and noticed for the first time that nearly everyone was fast asleep.

'*Tsk, tsk, tsk,*' he said very loudly and then even more loudly he went on, 'Wimbledon Wombles, I am going to America to see Cousin Yellowstone.'

'Why?' asked Bungo, waking up with a jerk.

'Because of all the difficulties I've been talking about. The world shortages of this and that,' snapped Great Uncle Bulgaria. 'If you'd been listening with half an ear you would have realised THAT.'

'Yes, yes, indeed,' said Madame Cholet, who had just come in from the kitchen. 'I'm sure Bungo did realise that. Tell me, Bulgaria, who is the lucky Womble you are taking with you to the United States?'

Great Uncle Bulgaria shuffled his notes together, cleared his throat and wished very much indeed that Madame Cholet hadn't asked that particular question at this particular moment. However, as all the Wombles had now woken up and, although they were rubbing their paws across their eyes, were looking fairly bright and interested, he had to reply. He looked over the top of his spectacles and then got out his second pair and put them on as well. He looked through both pairs and nearly every Womble felt his fur prickle in an uneasy sort of way.

'I'm taking with me a very bossy sort of young Womble,' said Great Uncle Bulgaria, 'a very bossy sort of young Womble, who is always asking far too many questions and thinking he knows far too many answers. But he doesn't. I think that working in the United States will do him a great deal of good. It'll stop him getting too big for his back paws for a start. And his name is . . .'

Great Uncle Bulgaria paused dramatically at this point, but unfortunately for him all the Wombles had now guessed who this helper was to be and they were all, even the very small Wombles from the Womblegarten, looking directly at Bungo, who was starting to shuffle around in his seat.

'I do believe it's young Mungo,' said Cousin Botany in his slow voice.

'No, no, no, Bungo,' snapped Great Uncle Bulgaria. 'Bungo, Bungo, BUNGO.'

Cousin Botany smiled in a vague sort of way, put a paw against his panama hat and shuffled out. Everybody else pushed and elbowed each other and giggled, except for the older Wombles and even they had to hide a smile or two. Bungo looked very hard at the ground and didn't know what to feel because, although he was starting to be very excited at the idea of going to America, he was also feeling a bit put down by Great Uncle Bulgaria's description of his character (which everybody else seemed to have recognised instantly!) and by being called Mungo.

It was left to Great Uncle Bulgaria to make everything seem all right again and, after just a very small hesitation, he did exactly that by saying briskly, 'Well, well, we're all rather overtired. Welcome back to our old burrow. I'm glad we're all together again, and I'm quite sure there are happy times ahead. Now off with the lot of you, quick sharp and get some sleep. Tomorrow's going to be a very busy day for all of us!'

It wasn't only tomorrow that was busy. It was all

the days that followed, for the Wombles soon discovered that their burrow was in a really shocking state. Doors wouldn't shut properly, there were leaks in the water pipes—one actually started going *drip-drip-drip* right beside Orinoco's bunk and he woke up with an awful start. Madame Cholet said it was the first time that she had seen Orinoco's face looking so clean for ages, which made everybody else laugh, but Orinoco didn't think it was at all funny and he was quite sharp and snappy for a bit.

'It's all work, work, WORK,' he grumbled. 'I shouldn't be at all surprised if I don't get a right case of falling fur from doing too much. It was bad enough getting that burrow under Hyde Park sorted out, but this is . . .'

'Oh, do shut up,' growled Tomsk, who had been put in charge of checking the luggage for Great Uncle Bulgaria and Bungo's trip to America. 'I've counted and counted bedsocks and shawls and the gifts we're sending all the Yellowstone Wombles, but the numbers keep on coming out different. Oh drat!'

'Shut up yourself,' said Orinoco and gave Tomsk a shove, which was a very bad mistake as Tomsk, of course, shoved right back and about twice as hard. The next moment the pair of them were rolling over and over with fur flying in all directions.

'STOP THAT!' ordered Tobermory, who had come into the dormitory at this most opportune moment, and he picked up a jug of water and emptied it over the pair of them. The two young Wombles gasped and shook themselves and shuffled their feet and then hurried back to work.

Luckily there's nothing like a good fight between friends to make things seem better, so Orinoco and Tomsk were all right for a bit, but Tobermory went '*Tsk, tsk, tsk*' under his breath and made yet another note in his little book.

'Fighting. Stop it! How?'

As Great Uncle Bulgaria had plenty of things on his mind already, Tobermory didn't bother him about this latest development—which was breaking out all over the burrow, as there always seemed to be a young Womble somewhere shoving or arguing or actually fighting another young Womble—but he did talk to Madame Cholet and Miss Adelaide who were having a nice, cosy chat round the kitchen table as they worked.

'*Tsk, tsk, tsk,*' said Miss Adelaide, carefully threading a needle.

'*Alors!*' exclaimed Madame Cholet, packing just one more toadstool truffle chocolate into a carton.

'It's all very well for you,' said Tobermory, '*you're* not left in charge while Bulgaria's off on his

25

holiday and . . .'

'Hardly a holiday, Tobermory,' said Miss Adelaide in exactly the tone of voice which had always made every Womble, whatever his age, suddenly feel rather young and silly. 'As I understand it, this is a most important Womble conference about worldwide shortages of this and that. Which reminds me, Tobermory, I'm running out of chalk for the blackboard, and material from which to make tidy-bags and ink. Furthermore we haven't much paper. I just thought I'd remind you!'

Tobermory got out his notebook yet again and wrote in it. Miss Adelaide and Madame Cholet exchanged glances and then Madame Cholet said gently, 'I have packed up all the truffles for the American Wombles and enough is enough. So now I make the hot drink. Perhaps a delicious bracken nightcap for you, Tobermory?'

'Yes, please,' said Tobermory. 'I really need something nice and soothing. I really do. I don't know how we're going to manage without Bulgaria . . .'

Everybody felt rather sad and cross and prickly when the day finally arrived on which Great Uncle Bulgaria and Bungo (who, for him, had got strangely quiet recently) were due to leave the burrow. All the Wombles lined up outside the front door and when Tobermory, looking very smart and most unlike himself in his chauffeur's cap, drove up in the Silver Womble, there was hardly a sound. Great Uncle Bulgaria cleared his throat and looked over and through his spectacles several times and then said in a very stern voice, 'Now then, young Wombles, stop looking so sorry

26

for yourselves. There's nothing to worry about as long as we all pull together. It's up to us Wombles to come to the rescue yet again, and I know we'll do it. How Human Beings would manage without us to help them I shall never understand, not if I live to be THREE hundred.

'Well, well, off we go then. Best of luck to you all and remember . . .' and Great Uncle Bulgaria raised one white paw, 'you're to do EXACTLY as Tobermory tells you, or I shall want to know the reason why! Ho-hum!'

For some strange reason these strict words made everybody feel much better and less sad, and the anxious looks gave way to smiles and some of the very small Wombles from the Womblegarten began to wave the flags which they had made for this very occasion.

Great Uncle Bulgaria smiled too and Bungo was almost going round in circles, he was being so bossy and self-important. And then Tobermory wound up the Silver Womble and it moved off very smoothly making just the faintest *tick-tock-tick-tock* sound as it sped across the Common, on to the road and vanished from sight.

'Elevenses,' said Madame Cholet, because when the car *did* disappear the smiling and waving stopped a bit suddenly.

'But it's only ten o'clock, you know,' said Wellington, coming out of a dream and looking at his enormous wristwatch.

'Haven't you ever heard of "tenses",' muttered Orinoco. 'They're FAR better than elevenses because they come an hour earlier and . . .'

'I know,' said Wellington, nodding, 'you're STARVING!'

'Mmmm,' agreed Orinoco, 'that's very clever of you. How did you guess? I say, I'm going to miss old Bungo a bit, aren't you? He may be a bossy sort of Womble, but he's all right really.'

But Wellington had already ambled away, with his paws clasped behind his back and his nose pointing towards the ground. He looked rather like Botany so that Tomsk, who didn't often notice that kind of thing, said in his rumbling voice, 'I'll tell you what—Wellington'll get as quiet and not-talking as Cousin Botany if he doesn't watch out. He's getting a bit like that already.'

'Don't suggest it,' said Orinoco with a shudder. 'I'll tell *you* what! Cousin Botany *missed his supper last night!*'

'He didn't!'

'He jolly well did! That's a very, very, VERY strange thing for a Womble to do. Move up, Tomsk, we're losing our place in the "tenses" queue.'

Alderney, who was in charge of the snack trolley, saw Orinoco's anxious face and waved and smiled and then began to push the trolley down the line of waiting, chattering Wombles so quickly that some of the chilled dandelion juice went flying in all directions.

A few drops reached Wellington, and, while he licked them off the back of his paw, he recalled what Great Uncle Bulgaria had said only twenty minutes ago.

'The Wombles to the rescue,' murmured Wellington. 'Yes, that's what we've got to do! We Wombles have got to stop all these shortages. Or find out how to deal with them anyway. That's a funny sort of problem to cope with, but we'll have to try and think of something. Now I wonder what I'd better invent FIRST . . .'

And away went Wellington talking to himself under his breath and with his head (as usual) so full of ideas of this-and-that that he never noticed that he was walking straight across the Common without bothering to keep clear of any Human Beings who might be about. As it happened there weren't many people actually out *walking*, but trundling down the slightly bumpy road which led to the Wimbledon Common Windmill was a large black van. On the side of the van were the letters 'WTV' . . .

'Where's Wellington got to?' asked Tomsk.

'I don't know,' said Orinoco. 'Look here, if you don't want another dandelion bun I'll eat it for you.'

'You've already had five!'

'Have I?' said Orinoco in such a surprised voice that Tomsk forgot all about the way in which Wellington had wandered off and began instead to count up dandelion buns on his paws.

All the others were busy talking and eating too, which is how Wellington wasn't missed for some time. Which was rather unfortunate as . . .

CHAPTER 4

THE GREY WOLF OF WIMBLEDON COMMON

Nobody missed Wellington for quite a long time. This was unusual as all Wombles keep an eye on each other and, besides being the most friendly of creatures, they are also most inquisitive and curious. Of course, if a Womble really feels he *must* have a bit of peace and quiet for a while, all the others do respect his views; but for a Womble to silently disappear, without anybody in the burrow noticing it, is practically unheard of. It only happened now because the burrow was all at sixes and sevens, what with Great Uncle Bulgaria and Bungo going to America and Tobermory away too, while he drove them on the first part of their journey.

It was Orinoco who first noticed that Wellington was missing and he only did so because Wellington—who was much better at getting up quickly—wasn't keeping a place for him in the breakfast queue.

'Hey,' said Orinoco, rubbing the sleep out of his eyes and nudging the small Womble ahead of him who was called Shansi. 'Where's Wellington, then?'

Shansi put her front paws together and shook her head sadly. She was rather shy as she had only just chosen her name, which was Chinese, and she was very much in awe of Wombles who had been working for some time as Orinoco had.

'Don't know,' she said in a low voice. 'Have not seen for many hours. So sorry.'

'Come to think of it, nor have I,' said Orinoco. 'Funny. Oh well, I suppose he'll turn up sooner or later. I wonder what's for breakfast?'

Shansi shook her head, because she didn't know the answer to that either, and she wondered if she would ever get used to being a working Womble. She had really enjoyed being in the Womblegarten and doing lessons like painting and sewing and pottery, but she was just discovering that those kind of jobs did not seem to exist once you left school. She had been sent to the kitchen to help Madame Cholet, but that marvellous cook, although very kind, had been so busy she hadn't had time to explain things properly, with the result that Shansi had mixed powdered clover into the nettle pie. It had given the pie a *most* unusual taste and even Orinoco had only just managed to finish his helping.

'No, no, no,' Madame Cholet had said, actually throwing her apron over her head and rocking backwards and forwards on her heels. 'I said powdered CLOVES, not clover. *Quel dommage!*'

31

A remark which had scared Shansi so much that she had not spoken for hours afterwards.

The next job that Shansi had been given was to go round with Alderney pushing the elevenses (sometimes tenses) trolley. Alderney hadn't had this job very long herself in actual fact, but the way she talked about it, it sounded as if she had been doing it for years and years. It was 'Do this, do that, oh do hurry up, Shansi, or we'll never get finished . . .' until poor Shansi got so flustered that she completely forgot to push her trolley into the Workshop, so that on that particular day Tobermory didn't get his hot dandelion juice—a drink to which he had really been looking forward.

'*Tsk, tsk, tsk*,' Tobermory had said. 'This just won't do, young Womble. You know the old saying, *A good hot drink helps a Womble think*. And I need all the help I can get at the moment, one way and another. What are we going to do with you? Hm?'

Shansi had wanted to suggest that she would like to go back to the Womblegarten, but she was too shy, so she had only hung her head and looked at the Workshop floor which was covered with tiny curls of wood shavings. They were rather pretty and they had a lovely, spicy smell.

'Well, well, well, off you go,' Tobermory had said, waving one grey paw at her. 'We'd better try you on tidying-up duty, I suppose. Report to the Workshop tomorrow for a tidy-bag. *Tsk, tsk, tsk*, I don't know what the world's coming to. Bulgaria off to America, doors sticking, Wombles bickering, hardly any ink left and now you forgetting my hot drink. *Tsk, tsk, tsk* . . .'

Shansi had felt worse than ever, as though everything that was going wrong in the burrow was all her fault, and she was the only Womble who hadn't managed to smile and wave when Great Uncle Bulgaria and Bungo set off on their great adventure. Now it was time for her to start on her third job and she was in such a state about it that she hardly took in a word Cousin Botany said, as he handed over a tidy-bag and showed her on the map which part of the Common she had to tidy up.

Shansi crept out of the burrow after her name had been ticked off in the Duty Book by Tomsk at the main front door, and then, with her heart going twice as fast as usual, she tiptoed through the bushes and out into the open. A blackbird went winging past her, giving its alarm call and Shansi nearly jumped out of her fur. She took a few more steps forward and then some more and finally she reached open ground.

It was a very nice morning and, as the sun was only just coming up and it was still fairly dark, there were no Human Beings about, although there was a steady stream of traffic on a distant road.

Shansi began to feel braver and rather less sad and worried and, when she actually saw some crumpled-up pieces of newspaper, she suddenly forgot to be careful and went running off across the grass to pick them up. To reach them she had to go round one small clump of trees and she was so excited that she never noticed that a strange, roundish, flattish object was hanging by a wire from one of the branches. However, it came to her notice very suddenly and rather painfully as she hit it, head-on. There was a loud CLONK and Shansi jumped round and round with her front paws clasped to her nose as she made a noise rather like

33

'*Waa-waa-waa-waa . . .*'

Several things now happened at once. The roundish object swung violently backwards and forwards until it got caught up in some brambles, a bright light appeared shining out of a caravan which was parked just beyond the trees (Shansi hadn't even realised it was there), there was the sound of raised voices and a dog started barking in the distance. An owl, high up in the tree, blinked its large eyes and then swooped down, avoided Shansi by the width of a feather and went silently on its way. Then quite suddenly first one bird and then another began to sing.

Shansi stopped going '*waa-waa-waa*' and she also stopped hopping about, because she was suddenly so scared by all this that she couldn't either make a sound or move a muscle. She didn't even stir when the light got much brighter as a door opened in the caravan and two Human Beings appeared, talking very angrily.

'I told you it was a rotten place to hang a microphone,' one of them said. 'I *told* you . . .'

'It wasn't a rotten place, it was the right place. The owl was in the tree all right and if that dog or person or whoever it was hadn't barged straight into the mike, we'd have got a splendid recording.'

'Well, we haven't . . .'

'I know THAT. Give me your torch . . .'

A thin beam of light travelled across the grass and just missed Shansi who was now starting to shiver, although she was still unable to move. Any minute now she would be discovered and probably captured and taken away, and she would be asked questions and all the Human Beings would take photographs of her and get her to tell them about

34

the Wombles. And Great Uncle Bulgaria and all the other Wombles would be furious and would never forgive her, because Wombles like to keep themselves to themselves as much as they possibly can.

All this flashed through Shansi's mind as quickly as the beam of light had leapt across the grey-green grass, but even so she just couldn't move because she felt exactly as if her back paws had been firmly glued to the ground. It was like one of those dreadful dreams when the more you try to run the less you can do so. And then, just as Shansi had shut her eyes as tight as they would go, and had given herself up as captured and lost to all the other Wombles for ever, a new and quite different noise shattered the dawn chorus of the birds.

It was a howl. It was a yell. It was a shriek. It rose and fell and was so dreadful that all the birds stopped singing and Shansi felt her fur stand right up on end. Even her ears went up. The men stopped only a mere five feet away from her and one of them said in a thick whisper, 'What on earth is THAT?'

'I   don't-don't-don't-don't-know-know-know-know,' replied the other man.

Everybody, even the birds, listened and once again the awful, scary, howling sound rang out.

'It's a wolf,' said the first man.

'It can't be!'

'It IS! A wolf on Wimbledon Common. Quick, quick, the microphone. This will make the story of the year! Hurry UP!'

The two men blundered right past Shansi and they began to try to get the roundish object out of the brambles where it had become all tangled up.

35

Before Shansi had quite realised what was happening a paw had gripped her arm and a familiar voice was hissing in her ear, 'Come ON. Quietly . . .'

And Shansi was pulled and pushed and bundled and prodded round the clump of trees where the two men were still arguing (and sucking their fingers because the brambles were very sharp) and down a slope where she lost her footing, so that she went head over heels like a small round furry ball until she came to rest in the shelter of some thick ferns. A slightly taller, skinnier ball of fur came to rest beside her and then the voice of Wellington said breathlessly, 'Honestly, Shansi, you should have been more careful! Still, thanks all the same.'

'Please,' said Shansi. 'Do not understand. Do not understand anything that is happening and want to go home.'

'Calm down,' said Wellington, taking off his large round spectacles and cleaning them on his scarf. 'We'll go back soon, when those men have stopped fiddling about with their old microphone. Gosh, I'm glad you came along. I'm starving. Just like Orinoco!'

Shansi still didn't understand, so she just sat there looking up at Wellington. As, up till now, Wellington had been the smallest of the working Wombles, he suddenly felt quite large and important with Shansi looking up at him. It was a new feeling and he enjoyed it.

'I've been trapped inside that old television caravan for ages,' he said, exaggerating just a bit.

'Taken prisoner?' breathed Shansi in horror.

'No, no, nothing like that. Only I thought I'd

36

explore inside it while those men were out on the Common hanging up their microphones, but one of them came back very quietly and I couldn't get out without being seen. So I had to hide and after that there was always one or other of 'em in there. It was quite interesting to listen to them—they're making a nature film for television all about the wildlife on the Common. You know, it's quite astonishing what they DON'T know. I was longing to tell them about Old Badger and those Wild Cats which have moved in, and the fox trail and . . .'

'The wolf!' said Shansi, her little eyes growing round as buttons as she remembered the awful up-and-down shriek. To her surprise Wellington started to chuckle and then to go 'Ho, ho, HO, HO' so loudly that he had to put both paws over his mouth.

'Wolf is nothing to laugh at,' said Shansi severely. Now that she had got over her fright and worry she was feeling rather cross and scratchy.

'Wolf IS something to laugh at when it happens to be me!' said Wellington, wiping the laughter tears off his spectacles. 'I was just slipping out of the caravan when I saw *you*, young Shansi, standing there with a petrified expression on your face. In another ten seconds those men would have seen you too and then there would have been trouble! So I did the first thing that came into my mind and howled like a wolf. I'll do it again if you like . . .'

'No, please. You make very good wolf. But no more. Thank you for rescuing me, Wellington.'

'That's all right. Well, it was a sort of mutual rescuing really, wasn't it? We rescued each other. Come on, it's all clear now and we'd better get back to the burrow.'

'Can't,' said Shansi. 'Have not tidied up anything. Have failed at every job. Cannot fail at this one too.'

'Oh, is that all that's worrying you?' said Wellington, politely ignoring the unhappy note in Shansi's small voice. 'Well, I know where there's an absolute load of rubbish. Those men dumped it. They kept on talking about the beauties of nature and looking after wildlife and all that sort of stuff, but they still put their dirty plastic cups and plates and old newspapers and tins and magazines and bits of cardboard and paper and . . .'

'Stop, stop, is enough!'

'I was only just getting going. They put it all in plastic bags and then shoved them under the bushes. Funny, really, when they were talking in such a bossy way about other people doing exactly the same thing. But then Human Beings are like that. I've noticed it before. This way, and keep quiet now, do . . .'

Everybody back at the burrow was astonished when they saw the two enormous bundles of rubbish that Shansi had brought back.

'Goodness you HAVE worked hard,' said Alderney, actually standing still for two seconds. 'You must be *ever* so hungry. Have a double daisy ice cream and a spoonful of clover cream.'

'Well done, little Beijing,' said Cousin Botany.

'Shansi,' said Shansi. 'Please, name is Shansi. Oh!'

'That's right,' agreed Cousin Botany. 'Shan-er? A very pretty name it is too. Hallo, what have you found there?'

It was a teacup without a handle. It was, or had

38

been, a very nice cup with flowers painted all round the outside rim and inside it too. Stamped on the bottom was: WTV. CHAIRMAN ONLY.

'Is lovely,' said Shansi, stroking it gently.

'You can keep it for your own special use,' said Cousin Botany. 'Go and wash it out carefully and then take it down to the canteen.'

Wellington was just finishing his third helping of pudding and being watched by a most respectful Orinoco.

'Never knew you could eat as well as that,' said Orinoco. 'Why, you're almost as good as me, young Wellington. Hallo, Shansi, coming to join us? Good, sit down. Watching Wellington has made me feel quite peckish. Think I'll have a little something just to keep me going . . .'

Off ambled Orinoco and Wellington put his spoon and fork neatly together and blew out his cheeks. Shansi leant forward and said in her quiet little voice, 'You were hungry as wolf, yes?'

'That's right,' said Wellington, 'but we'd better keep quiet about it. Great Uncle Bulgaria'd have a fit if he ever found out . . . Right, young Shansi?'

'Right!'

For the first time since she had left the Womblegarten, Shansi decided that perhaps being a working Womble wasn't going to be too bad after all. Wellington was feeling happy and contented too. He'd had a most interesting twenty-four hours as a semi-prisoner and had picked up all kinds of ideas. The two young Wombles, in fact, felt very pleased with themselves. They might have felt rather differently if they had known that seven days later Great Uncle Bulgaria, in the spacious, air-conditioned burrow which was run by Cousin

39

Yellowstone, would be reading a certain newspaper cutting. It was headed:

WOLF SEEN ON WIMBLEDON COMMON
A DANGEROUS GREY WOLF OF CONSIDERABLE SIZE
WAS SPOTTED ON WIMBLEDON COMMON AT DAWN
YESTERDAY BY TELEVISION DIRECTOR . . .

Great Uncle Bulgaria read through the cutting three times and then folded his white paws together and said, 'How strange. How *very* strange. *I* have never heard of a wolf on the Common and if I have never heard of it, then it probably does NOT exist. I wonder what is going on. I think perhaps that I had better write a letter . . .'

Great Uncle Bulgaria looked at the range of pencils, biros, and pens which had been put out for his use, went '*tsk, tsk, tsk*' under his breath, and started to write . . .

CHAPTER 5

GREAT UNCLE BULGARIA SENDS A LETTER

From: BULGARIA COBURG WOMBLE C/O COUSIN YELLOWSTONE WOMBLE, USA

To: THE WOMBLES OF WIMBLEDON

Dear Wombles,

You will no doubt be pleased to hear that Bungo and I have arrived safe and well after a very smooth crossing.

Our American cousins are most kindly and considerate, if a trifle talkative, and their burrow is very efficiently run, although I could wish for a little less ice with every cold drink. Many other senior Wombles have already arrived and the Conference on World Shortages is due to start soon. I have no doubt that it will be most instructive and, we trust, PRODUCTIVE! I hope most sincerely that all my

41

Wombles of Wimbledon are also thinking up ideas which may help the problem of shortages. Before I close I would like to say two things. First, that Bungo wishes to send his warmest regards to you all, especially he informs me, to Tomsk, Orinoco and Wellington. And secondly, that I should be most interested to learn more about the Common's latest newcomer. I refer to the Grey Wolf. May I remind you, young Wombles, you can cry wolf once too often if you're not careful!

Kindest best wishes to you all.
GREAT UNCLE BULGARIA.

After this remarkable letter had been read aloud to everybody by Tobermory, Wellington had the distinct feeling that, although he was thousands of miles away, Great Uncle Bulgaria was looking directly at *him*, so he slipped out of the playroom and went off to do something nice and ordinary like swimming in Queen's Mere with Tomsk.

'Funny about that wolf,' said Tomsk, doing a perfect running dive. He went smoothly into the water and emerged halfway down the Mere, shaking the water out of his round little eyes as he went on, 'I didn't know there was a wolf on the Common.'

'Mmmmmm,' said Wellington, in a voice which could have meant anything.

'Perhaps there never was a wolf,' remarked Orinoco, who had found a comfortable spot beside the Mere for a snooze. He looked out from under the brim of his hat and stared very hard at Wellington, who had begun to whistle in an offhand sort of way. 'I bet it's never heard of again

42

anyway,' went on Orinoco with a fat wheezy chuckle as he pulled the hat down over his face and settled back for a nice thirty winks. It was only thirty that he really felt he wanted as he hadn't been working all that hard recently. Human Beings were still dumping rubbish on the Common, but there wasn't quite so much of it these days and, what was really a bit worrying, they were getting almost mean about the food that they were throwing away.

Orinoco scratched his stomach and sighed as he recalled the Good Old Days when an alert Womble might find an almost complete picnic meal left behind on a bench. Or half a packet of toffees. Or perhaps two or three bananas. Or a tin of biscuits. Or . . .

'Oh dear,' said Orinoco and rolled over on to his stomach to try and stop it rumbling. Now, up to this particular moment, Orinoco hadn't really thought one little bit about all the things Great Uncle Bulgaria had said about shortages of this and that, but now it suddenly came into his mind that the 'this and that' might refer to food. It was as if a thick grey cloud had floated across the sun.

'Oh my,' said Orinoco, sitting bolt upright, 'surely we could never run out of FOOD? Not like we nearly did in that very bad winter! [See *The Wombles.*] No, we're quite safe now since Cousin Yellowstone showed Tobermory how to build a Deep Freeze. All the same perhaps I will just stroll back to the burrow and have a word with Madame Cholet . . .'

It started as a stroll, then it became a walk and then a trot and finally a scamper.

'Whatsermatter with Orinoco?' asked Tomsk,

flipping head over paws in a perfect somersault.

'Probably being chased by a bee,' replied Wellington, spluttering and thrashing about, because he wasn't half as good at swimming as Tomsk was. 'I say, Tomsk, old Womble, I've just had a smashing idea. Those men I met . . .'

'What men?'

'Oh, just men. They were sort of working on the Common. Don't interrupt, there's a good Womble, or I'll forget what my idea is. These men were saying that there isn't enough oil to go round.'

Tomsk was about to ask 'go round what?' but he decided it was probably better to keep quiet.

'So I think we should drill for oil,' said Wellington. 'These men said . . .'

'They seem to talk a lot. Have they got names? It's easier when people have names. Don't you remember how difficult it was sometimes in the Womblegarten before we'd chosen our names out of Great Uncle Bulgaria's atlas? Miss Adelaide would say, "Stand up that young Womble who was talking" and we'd *all* stand up. Or at least nearly all . . .'

'Perhaps that's *why* she did it,' said Wellington. 'Oh, please, PLEASE, do keep quiet a sec. Yes, the men called each other John and Terry, and they were talking about there not being enough petrol and oil and yes, I do know that WOM I doesn't run on petrol, but Tobermory was saying we needed oil in the burrow for oiling all those squeaking hinges and things. So you and me are going to build an oil rig and we're going to drill for oil under Queen's Mere. What do you think of that?'

But Tomsk was beyond saying anything. He just stood in the shallow water at the side of Queen's

44

Mere with his mouth slightly open and with a drip on the end of his nose. And then he did a perfect sideways dive and vanished with hardly a ripple.

'I knew you'd agree,' said Wellington happily. 'Now I wonder how *exactly* one builds an oil rig . . .'

Back at the burrow Orinoco was following Madame Cholet round the kitchen, almost treading on her heels as he said anxiously, 'But I say, look here, Madame Cholet, do you really mean that we might RUN OUT OF FOOD?'

'Not run out, young Womble, but regard this if you please,' and Madame Cholet led the way into one of the larders and threw open a cupboard door. It was a very clean and neat cupboard with just one line of small plastic pots in it. 'Bramble jelly,' announced Madame Cholet.

'Lovely. Um. DEE-licious. Quite my favourite next to dock or perhaps oak apple. Although I must admit I'm quite partial to sweet acorn and then there's . . .'

'It's *all* the bramble jelly that is left,' said Madame Cholet and shut the door with a click which sent a shiver straight up Orinoco's back.

'Why?' he asked in a very small voice.

'Because a lot of the brambles were cut back last year to provide more open space for the Human Beings. Regard further, young Womble.' And Madame Cholet, who had been worrying away at the back of her own mind about food, suddenly began to talk very fast. It was such a relief to be able to put all her fears into words, and Orinoco was quite old enough now to face up to some of the real difficulties of the world.

45

And off went Madame Cholet to the next larder to show Orinoco that there were only two bins of chopped dried nettles.

'Those were cut back last year too,' she said, 'and it's not only us Wombles who will miss the nettles. The butterflies do too. Have you noticed that there are fewer butterflies about this year? No, I don't suppose you have. But when I was a young Womble there used to be hundreds of them, like flying flowers all over the Common. Then Human Beings started filling the air with nasty fumes and using those horrid sprays in their gardens and the butterflies began to vanish. It is very sad. *Oui?*'

'*Oui*, yes, rather,' said Orinoco miserably. He was wishing very much that he had never begun asking questions because everything was turning out so much nastier than he had imagined. In fact he was now starting to imagine himself, and all the other Wombles, just fading away and becoming as thin as Human Beings. And a thin Womble is very nearly impossible to imagine, which goes to show how upset Orinoco was becoming.

However, Madame Cholet was now fairly into her stride and she took hold of Orinoco by one ear and made him come with her on a grand inspection of all the larders and even the Deep Freeze which was humming away quietly to itself at the far end of the burrow.

'Well, that's not too bad,' said Orinoco, brightening up just a tiny bit as he gazed down through the icy misty atmosphere at the heaps of small plastic packets of this and that.

'It's all last year's stock,' said Madame Cholet. 'And where, I ask myself, will next year's food come from, hm?'

'The Common?'

'Foolish one! All the time Human Beings cut back, cut down, uproot all kinds of bushes and trees and plants. And why? Because they seem to think they need more grass. And for what do they use the grass? For walking on, sunbathing on, bicycling on. All these things are very well in their way, but the ground should be fed and dug and fed and planted and used for growing. If matters continue like this we Wombles will be living on nothing but grass. And what can I—a cook of some distinction, I think you will agree—'

'Rather!'

'*Merci*. What can I do with merely grass? Bread, pancakes, a few puddings and mixes, perhaps a little ice cream and sauce, but nothing more. And Wombles are not sheep. To live on a diet of grass will be very bad for us. We shall all get falling fur, mark my words.'

47

'What—what,' said Orinoco, swallowing pain-fully, 'what's to be done, Madame Cholet?'

Madame Cholet's shoulders rose to her ears and she spread her front paws wide in a gesture of 'I don't know, you tell me'.

'Oh lor,' muttered Orinoco. 'I say, look here, Madame Cholet, don't get too upset, please. I—I'll think of something to help. I promise.'

And Orinoco ducked his head a couple of times and then went hurrying off. Madame Cholet watched him go and then picked up an edge of her frilly apron and wiped the corners of her eyes.

'He starts to grow up, little fat Orinoco,' she said to herself. 'For once he worries about other Wombles as well as himself. *Alors*, I hope he—or one of us—*will* think of something. Well, now that I am here, I had better just check on the shredded toadstools and tree fungi. There's nothing like work for making you forget your worries after all . . .'

And Madame Cholet blew her nose on a small lace handkerchief which had CHOLET embroidered on one corner, and got out a notebook and pencil from her pocket and began to count up the bottles, pots and packets that she had left in all her larders.

Orinoco went off in a very thoughtful mood, his paws clasped behind his back and his chin sunk on his chest. He was so intent on the awful problem of Not Enough Food that he walked straight past Alderney who was going off with a very patched tidy-bag over her arm.

'Hallo,' said Alderney.

'Mmmf,' said Orinoco.

'Oh, very well, if that's how you feel,' said

Alderney in a most superior voice. 'I *was* going to ask you if you'd come and look for lichens we could make into savoury spreads, but if that's the way you feel I shan't bother.'

'Don't pick too much or there may not be enough left,' said Orinoco, sounding so stern it could have been Great Uncle Bulgaria speaking. Away he went, leaving Alderney staring after him till she saw Shansi coming down the passage carrying a bulging tidy-bag with what looked like several sticks poking out of the top.

'Hey, hallo,' said Alderney, thinking as she spoke how friendly she was being to a new working Womble, 'you can come on a lichen hunt with me if you like.'

Shansi stopped dead, not looking at all delighted at this gracious invitation. In fact she appeared to be almost dismayed. However, being the most polite Womble probably in the whole world, she then put her front paws together, ducked her head twice and said in a soft voice, 'Most kind. Most gracious. Regret cannot accept as have other employment. Please excuse.'

And Shansi, with yet another polite nod of her head, hurried past Alderney and out of the burrow before that young Womble could get her breath back. When she did, she said to nobody in particular, for there was nobody else about apart from Miss Adelaide who was just coming out of the Womblegarten with a worried frown on her grey furry forehead, 'Well, really! Not that I care! I don't care AT ALL!'

And most regrettably Alderney then stamped out of the burrow and actually kicked the doorpost as she passed it. A shower of fine dust fell softly

49

from the wood and Miss Adelaide said, '*Tsk, tsk, tsk*. What is happening to this burrow! Nothing runs smoothly or pleasantly any more. Even my Womblegarten are not the happy young Wombles they used to be and it's no wonder when the working Wombles set them such a bad example. The sooner Bulgaria returns the better it will be for all of us!'

Miss Adelaide, her back very straight indeed, went off to have a word with her old friend Madame Cholet, passing as she did so the Workshop where Tobermory, for once in his very long life, was facing a problem with which even he couldn't cope.

There just wasn't enough wood, seasoned or otherwise, with which to make all the new doors and fittings that the burrow needed.

'Short of going and sawing some trees down on the Common,' muttered Tobermory, 'I don't know what's to be done and that's a fact. I knew there'd be trouble ahead, but I never imagined anything like this. The sooner Bulgaria gets back the better. Now then, where was that piece of planking I had put by? Dratted Human Beings, I'd let 'em stew in their own silliness if I had my way. Now there's a strange thing, some of the old cups have vanished from the back storeroom. Who'd want *them*, I wonder!'

So there they all were, muttering and grumbling to themselves about this and that. It was as if everything in the Wimbledon burrow was boiling up and up and up and then at any minute there would be a tremendous rumble and roar and the Trouble would start.

The strange thing was that it was the quietest

50

Womble of them all who would start matters really
humming . . .

CHAPTER 6

COUSIN BOTANY'S SECRET

Wellington read up everything he could in the library about building oil rigs but, as this was very little indeed, he wasn't much the wiser by the end of the next few days. All he was certain about was the way the rigs actually looked, but what they did underneath the North Sea, or anywhere else for that matter, remained a mystery.

'Never mind,' Wellington said to Tomsk, who hadn't thought of minding anyway as he wasn't at all sure what they were supposed to be doing. 'I expect that once we've built the rig-thing we'll know how it works. OK?'

'Mm. It won't upset the swimming, will it? Or the skating? I mean, if it's a nice cold winter we might get some good skating. I like skating,' said Tomsk who was good at absolutely every game and sport and who had once gone round the Wimbledon golf course in Par. (Great Uncle

Bulgaria had told Tomsk that this was what he had done and that it was something of which to be proud. Tomsk hadn't quite worked out yet just what *exactly* these mysterious words meant.)

'No, of course not,' said Wellington. 'Well, that is, Terry and John did say something about oil companies spoiling the environment. But they meant *ever* so big oil rigs with lots and lots of Human Beings working on them, and this rig is just going to have you and me. Now look at this picture.'

'It's a sort of tower,' said Tomsk after a long pause. 'Isn't it?'

'Yes, and we're going to make one like it.'

'What with?'

'Well, I think it's supposed to be steel, but we don't get much of that dumped on the Common, so I thought perhaps we'd do ours with what we could find and pick up. Come ON.'

Wellington was getting quite bossy now that Bungo was in America and so couldn't push everybody about. Added to which there's nothing like an even younger and more shy Womble such as Shansi being grateful, to make a Womble such as Wellington get rather grand ideas about himself. So for the next few days (when they weren't doing some tidying-up work or sleeping or playing games or helping Tobermory, Madame Cholet or Miss Adelaide or adding their two lines to the long letters which were being sent regularly to America), Tomsk and Wellington picked up bits of this and that and collected bits of that and this until they had enough pieces with which to build a rig.

It was a most difficult thing to do, and as neither

53

Wellington nor Tomsk were particularly handy with their paws, they kept hitting themselves with hammers and losing screws and even, when matters got somewhat out of hand, hitting each other. But Wellington was absolutely determined to make a rig and Tomsk felt that Wellington probably really did know deep down what this strange business was all about and should be helped.

'A shortage of oil means a lot more toil,' muttered Tomsk as he sucked his grazed knuckles and tried to ease the ache in his back.

'It doesn't look bad, does it?' said Wellington, gazing proudly at their handiwork. 'I mean, considering what it's made of!'

It was indeed a most remarkable construction of bits of fencing, pieces of plastic, some iron railings, string, wire, rope, a plastic hosepipe, the central shaft of an umbrella and a bicycle pump. It certainly resembled a miniature oil rig and its two inventor-builders thought it was beautiful. To anybody else it might have appeared a very strange thing indeed.

'It's not half bad,' agreed Tomsk, quite forgetting his hurt knuckles. 'What do we do now?'

Wellington had been slightly dreading this point, because it is one thing to copy something you've seen in a photograph and quite another to get the something actually working. He had a hazy idea of the principle of drilling for oil; that is, that first they would have to make a deep hole and then they would pump up whatever was at the bottom of the hole. Only, there can be a very big gap between the idea of what should be done and actually doing it. Wellington saw that gap opening up before him at this moment and swallowed nervously. Tomsk, who believed that Wellington was even more clever than Great Uncle Bulgaria and could therefore do *anything*, watched his friend with round unblinking eyes and waited to be told what to do next.

'We get it going,' said Wellington in a high squeaky voice. 'It's a lovely day for it.' It was a lovely day from the Wombles' point of view, as it was raining steadily and there was a nice cold east wind. These weather conditions meant that no Human Beings would be out on the Common so that Wellington and Tomsk would be able to launch the rig undisturbed. 'Come on.'

Very gently they loaded the rig on to a wheelbarrow and then, as quietly as possible, they pushed it through the burrow from the far end of the Workshop where they had built it. The front door creaked and groaned and almost stuck as it was opened and a shower of sawdust drifted out of the hinges, but Wellington and Tomsk were in too much of an excited dither to notice this.

Once clear of the burrow they made for Queen's Mere as fast as they could. The weight of the rig made them stagger and slip but at last they reached the water where the ducks, who didn't mind the weather, were placidly diving for food.

'Now we . . .' said Wellington and stopped because he suddenly remembered a bit in the newspaper he had read about 'floating oil rigs out to their destination'. The destination of this particular rig was only a question of yards away, but no matter how hard and fast he and Tomsk swam, carrying the rig between them, it would sink (because of the iron bars) within feet of the shore.

'Drat!' said Wellington and made the furious face which meant he was really thinking furiously. Tomsk watched him respectfully. 'Hold on a tick,' said Wellington and scuttled off the bank in the direction of the burrow.

Tomsk, who really had been working extremely hard and was therefore quite tired, decided that he might have a bit of a rest in among the dripping bushes and ferns. He settled himself in comfortably, folded his paws across his stomach and sighed contentedly.

That Wellington might be rather a small sort of Womble and was not good at games at all—look at that time when they'd tried a round of golf some while ago—but he was awfully good at Thinking. And Thinking was something which Tomsk found quite difficult to get to grips with. He didn't have to think when he hit a tennis ball, or did a perfect running three-quarter turn and flip dive, or learnt to ski almost up to championship standards in a couple of hours. He did all those sort of things without . . .

Tomsk's pleasant thoughts were interrupted as his sharp ears caught the sound of a twig snapping and then a faint thud of feet followed by the ghost of a worried sigh. Inch by inch Tomsk raised himself out of the bracken and saw a small, tubby, grey-white figure wearing an apron and a battered straw hat trotting down the slope towards the Mere. It was Cousin Botany. That mysterious, lonely sort of Womble who seemed to live in a world of his own.

Botany was certainly being most mysterious at the moment, as he was actually wading into the water until it reached his knees and then, from out

56

of his apron pocket, he produced a sort of tube, one end of which he put up to his eye and the other he directed to the surface of the water.

An inquisitive duck came swimming up to see what was happening and the ripples that it made sloshed against the end of the tube and made Botany glance up.

'Stupid bird,' he said crossly and, wiping the end of the tube on the bib of his apron, he returned to the path looking more thoughtful than ever, and if anything, sadder and more worried than he had done before. It was a very funny sort of way to behave and Tomsk lay back quietly for he felt that probably Cousin Botany didn't want to talk to anybody at the moment. Not that he often appeared to want to talk to anyone. It was all very strange and Tomsk was still thinking about it in a muzzy sort of way when Wellington came crashing back with two enormous pieces of white polystyrene under his arms and a great grin on his face.

'Floats,' he said breathlessly. 'And I'll tell you what else we need, only I couldn't carry it as well. A bucket.'

'A bucket! What for? I say, Wellington, I saw . . .'

'A bucket for the oil, of course. I say, Tomsk, this is jolly exciting, isn't it? I mean finding oil in the bottom of Queen's Mere. Great Uncle Bulgaria and Tobermory and everybody'll be ever so pleased. Get a move on and get a bucket, there's a good Womble. My specs have misted over . . .'

'OK, but look here, Wellington, I saw . . .'

But Wellington, who was getting quite carried away by his own marvellous ideas, only waved an

57

impatient paw, so Tomsk gave up trying to explain about Cousin Botany and went running as fast as he could (which was very fast indeed with his elbows into his side and his chin up) back to the burrow. In record-breaking time he was back with a bucket, just as Wellington had managed to get the rig balanced on the two pieces of polystyrene.

'Great,' said Wellington. 'The oil will be pumped, by the bicycle pump, into the bucket which I'll tie on here. It'll travel up this tube here, shoot up—I think it's called a gusher or something—and then we watch it as it all comes down again. OK?'

'Ah,' said Tomsk, who had got lost about the third word.

It was really quite difficult floating the rig out to the middle of the Mere because the ducks would keep coming to investigate what was happening and the more they swam round and made ripples, the more the rig rocked about and very nearly came off its floats.

'When . . . when I say one, two, three, go,' said Wellington breathlessly, 'we both pull our floats out from under the rig at the same time. We've got to do it carefully though, otherwise the rig might tip over.'

'What's it supposed to do?' asked Tomsk.

'Sink,' snapped Wellington, who could hardly see anything by this time, as his spectacles had not only steamed over with excitement, but were also covered in water, so that he felt as if he was trying to look through paper.

'But how can it work if it sinks?' asked Tomsk, who was getting more and more muddled by the whole project.

'IT'S SUPPOSED TO SINK. Are you ready? One, two, three—*puuuuuuull.*'

The rig sank all right. The moment the floats were pulled from under it, down it went with a gurgling sound until with a *clunk-clonk* it hit the mud on the bottom, leaving about half of itself sticking out of the water. A great many large, flat bubbles rose slowly to the surface and swilled about for a moment or two and then burst. There was a distinctly rich, unusual smell.

'Oil,' said Wellington, 'that's oil! We've hit oil!'

'Are you sure?' asked Tomsk, who was treading water and holding his nose, because if this was what oil smelt like he wasn't at all sure that he wanted to know more about it.

' 'Course I am. And it can't be much below the bottom of the lake either. Now we'd better start the drilling bit. I want you to dive down, because you're much better at diving than me, to spin the umbrella shaft. That will go down and down into the oil bed and then you start working the bicycle pump so that oil comes up to gush. It's very good fun, isn't it, Tomsk?'

'Yeees,' said Tomsk a shade doubtfully, 'but, Wellington . . .'

'Go on, go *on. Please.*' Wellington waved both his front paws at once, his blue and black cap right over one eye and his face smiling from ear to ear.

'Oh, very well,' said Tomsk and took a tremendous deep breath before he dived, which is how he missed everything that happened next.

Wellington was still clutching on to the oil rig to keep it steady as, despite the iron railings, it did tend to tilt a bit, when suddenly there was the most extraordinary and fur-lifting sound from the bank.

It was a roar, a bellow and a cry of anguish and it was far, far worse than the wolf noise which Wellington had made some days before.

Wellington's fur stood up in prickles and he just managed to keep his grip on the oil rig as he looked over his shoulder and saw a small, round, grey-white Womble, wearing a straw hat and an apron, come tearing down the slope with a fishing net in one hand and a home-made telescope in the other.

'Vandals, wreckers, destroyers,' roared Cousin Botany. 'What are you doing, eh? Oh, leave off, leave off, do! All my years and years and YEARS of work all gone for nothing! Wait till I gets my paws on you, just wait!'

'But, Cousin Botany,' said Wellington, 'I don't understand. What's the matter? What are you so upset about? What have we done that's wrong?'

'That's what you've done,' roared Cousin Botany, pointing with one trembling paw at the oil rig which had now settled down firmly with its top half out of the water. Bubbles were still bursting on the surface of the Mere and the strange, juicy smell was becoming more and more pronounced. 'That's what you've done, young Womble. Ruined all the life's work of me, Botany Womble. Everything was a-going so well, apart from a trouble or two, and now it's done for and I holds you to blame . . .'

'I still don't understand . . .'

'No, nor ever will now that all's ruined. All them years ago out in Australia I had this idea. I went down to the harbour to see about stores and as I looked over the side of this ship what did I see? I see all these lovely little rich green plants a-

60

growing under the water. Well, I says to myself, Botany Womble, this is a right rich country with plenty of ground for growing, but one day maybe things could change and those troublesome Human Beings, silly creatures, will use up a lot of land for their houses and this and that. And then what will happen to growing land? Eh?'

'I don't know,' whispered Wellington, whose eyes were now as round as pennies as Cousin Botany pointed one silver-grey paw at him as if it was entirely his, Wellington's, fault that all this was happening.

'I'll tell you,' said Cousin Botany. 'I'll tell you, young Womble. It's what's happening here on this very Wimbledon Common. There'll be a lot of open space and the trees and bushes and plants'll be cut right back and *there won't be enough food to go round*. And there's me, Botany Womble, as has built or tried to build Womble feeding grounds under the water. AND YOU'VE GONE AND RUINED 'EM ALL!'

And to Wellington's horror old Cousin Botany took off his ancient straw hat, put it down on the ground and began to jump up and down on it as he said, 'That's that then. All my work done and over with. I'll not work for this burrow no more. I won't, I won't, I WON'T!'

'I say, Wellington,' said Tomsk, slowly surfacing among the bubbles, 'there's something very sort of funny about the bottom of the Mere. Something sort of funny which I don't think is oil . . .'

'Oh dear, oh dear, oh dear,' said Wellington. 'OH DEAR!'

CHAPTER 7

TOMSK HAS AN IDEA

Botany was a most unusual Womble for until now he had been a non-talker, but once he saw the Womble-made oil rig and the greasy bubbles on the water he changed completely, because he really did think that all his careful work had been destroyed. He stopped being slow and quiet and thoughtful and became very angry indeed. He dashed into Queen's Mere with a turn of speed surprising in a Womble of his age, and grabbed hold of the astonished Tomsk by the scruff of his neck and dragged him out of the water. Then Cousin Botany gripped on to Wellington's fur—which wasn't difficult as it was all standing on end—and he tugged and pulled and argued the two young Wombles back to the burrow and down the main corridor and into the Workshop. There Tobermory was wearily mending a brace and bit while trying to think of the answer to the woodworm which had attacked all the doors in the burrow.

'Here, what's all this?' he demanded, looking rather astonished as well he might for the three muddy, dripping Wombles really did make a most unusual picture.

'This,' said Botany, his voice quite hoarse with anger and breathlessness, 'this is two of your precious young Wombles as have ruined all my years of work. You do with them as you will, Tobermory, seeing as you're in charge, but if I had my way I'd send them to Coventry for THREE MONTHS.'

The threat of not being allowed to talk to anybody for three months was so awful, indeed unheard of, that both Tomsk and Wellington sagged at the knees, their mouths open and their eyes rolling. Botany gave them a good shake which sent plops of mud going in all directions, and also made Wellington find his tongue.

'It's not fair,' he said, trying to twist out of Botany's firm grip. 'We didn't know we were doing anything wrong. You never told anybody NOT to go digging in Queen's Mere!'

'Digging in the *Mere*?' said Tobermory, wondering if he was going quite dotty or having a weird sort of dream.

'For oil.'

'Underwater.'

'Wet farming.'

Tobermory took a deep breath, shut his eyes for a second and felt for his carpenter's stool and sat down with a bump. He had never before wished more devoutly that Bulgaria was down the corridor in his study reading *The Times*. Bulgaria would

have sorted out this trouble in ten minutes flat,
starting off by looking over and then through two
pairs of spectacles in that particular way he had.
But Bulgaria was thousands of miles away at the
dratted Conference, and Tobermory didn't wear
spectacles. Instead he reached over for the inter-
burrow-phone, blew down it in such a piercing way
that Orinoco, who was on duty, nearly fell off his
seat in the telephone exchange, and asked for four
hot, extra sweet bracken juices to be sent to the
Workshop *immediately*.

Tobermory then put his grey paws together,
looked over the top of them and said sternly,
'Please compose yourselves, Wombles. As soon as
the trolley arrives we will have a drink and THEN,
starting with Cousin Botany, we will discuss
matters quietly.'

It was so unlike Tobermory to talk like this—it
was almost as if it was Great Uncle Bulgaria sitting
at the carpenter's bench—that everybody did

exactly as they were told, and while avoiding each other's eyes, they brushed down their fur and, in the case of Botany, tried to take some of the dents out of his battered panama hat.

Of course, all the other Wombles knew that Something was Up, what with the shouting and the muddy pawprints all up the corridor and the way the Workshop door had been slammed. So they hung about in little groups, whispering and feeling rather uneasy because everything in the burrow seemed uncomfortable these days. And there was an awful draught from the front door which no longer shut properly. There was a clatter and a swish of trolley tyres and Alderney came fairly trotting out of the kitchen with her cap over one eye and the ties of her apron flying out behind her. She was scared and excited at the same time because all the others were looking at her, which made her feel important, but when she cautiously knocked on the Workshop door and Tobermory's voice barked, 'COME', Alderney could have turned and run for one pin, let alone two.

However, she'd had her orders so in she went, trembling so much that the urn full of delicious bracken juice went *clatter-clatter-clatter* on the trolley. And she looked so funny with her cap now descending over both eyes, while she tried to stop the clattering, that Wellington forgot about being hard done by and started to chuckle. That set Tomsk off, and as he'd got the most marvellous deep 'HO, HO, HO' laugh, *that* began to make Tobermory's mouth twitch so that he was soon going 'Heh-heh-heh'. Cousin Botany held on to his upset dignity for a little longer and then he began to make little grunting noises which was his way of

65

laughing.

Alderney, her nose very much up in the air, poured out the hot drinks, but after a second or two even she couldn't help giggling. There's nothing like laughter for getting rid of hurt feelings and within a very few minutes, Tobermory had learnt all about Cousin Botany's extraordinary experiments which he had started so many years ago.

'Underwater farming,' said Wellington, his eyes beginning to shine behind his spectacles, 'but isn't it very difficult? I know we can hold our breath for a long time, but even so . . .'

'That's the least of my problems, that is,' replied Cousin Botany. 'First off I never did think any of you'd take my idea serious, which is why I did keep so quiet about it, see?'

Everybody nodded and Cousin Botany went on, 'Then there was all the trouble of finding plants as we could eat and enjoy as would let themselves be grown underwater. Terrible times I had there, and those dratted Human Beings would keep throwing rubbish into the water. Poisonous stuff some of it too. Although I will say,' Botany added grudgingly, 'they're not quite as bad as they used to be. Then there was the ducks. I had to grow plants as *they* wouldn't fancy, otherwise they'd have had the lot. Greedy birds.'

'And how far have you got now?' asked Tobermory.

'Well, the food's there all right, but 'tis the harvesting, like, as young Wellington says. Planting out ain't so simple, neither.'

The others, who had all started to perk up, now felt not quite so optimistic. If the food was going to

66

be so difficult to grow, was it going to be the answer to their problems after all?

'What about my oil rig?' said Wellington, making his dreadful thinking face. 'Couldn't we use that?'

'For harvesting, yes. But what about the planting out, then?'

Tobermory, Cousin Botany and Wellington all began to think and to draw little diagrams on bits of paper while they talked between themselves. They forgot all about Tomsk who hadn't really followed a great deal of what had happened anyway. He had been hoping to get in a quick round of golf if the good (that is, cold, pouring wet) weather held up. Of course, if it rained too much it might have a bad effect on the course and he would have to add a bit more power to his drives with all that water lying about. Now if only the water could be drained away it would mean he could play golf in a real old downpour.

Tomsk scratched the last of the mud off his fur, turned some ideas over in his head slowly and then, being a Womble of few words, said simply, 'Do your underwater plants somewhere else.'

'Oh, yes, where? In puddles?' said Wellington, who was sorry that his beautiful oil rig wasn't going to be any use after all. Tobermory had just gently but firmly explained that a rig had to go down thousands of feet to strike oil, and that nine times out of ten they didn't find it anyway.

'Under the Common,' said Tomsk, one eye on the clock.

'In the *burrow*?'

'Sort of. In tanks. Plenty of water about when it rains. Too much.'

'Oh, Tomsk, don't be . . .' Wellington began crossly when Cousin Botany suddenly threw his hat into the air and actually lifted the skirt of his apron and danced a few steps.

' 'Tis it, 'tis it, you great gormless Womble,' he said, while the others stared at him. 'I couldn't see the tanks for the pond, so I couldn't.'

'Tanks, rainwater, drainage . . .' Tobermory wrote rapidly on his list which had now reached No. 39. 'Pipes. Inlets. Outlets. Lighting. A lot of help will be needed to find all the necessary equipment. All paws to the Underwater Plough! *That'll* keep 'em busy and stop 'em fighting. Hurrah!' And Tobermory put the pencil back behind his ear and really smiled properly for the first time since Great Uncle Bulgaria had gone to America.

'You don't really think it'd work, do you?' asked Wellington, feeling thoroughly put out now as he had never before considered Tomsk to be a Womble of Ideas.

'It'll have to,' said Tobermory. 'Now there's a lot to be done. First off . . . yes, yes, Tomsk, what is it? Stop waving your great paw about like that.'

'Can I go now, please,' said Tomsk. 'I mean if we're not oil rigging or anything else for an hour or two. Golf.'

'Yes, yes, yes. Off you go and play at least three rounds. You deserve it. Thank you, Tomsk.'

'*Three rounds!* Yes, Tobermory. Not at all,' said Tomsk who hadn't the least idea what he was being thanked for. First you were in trouble and then you were out of it. It was all most confusing and he'd better disappear fast before his luck changed yet again.

68

So Tomsk disappeared with Tobermory's following words ringing in his ears, 'And send Shansi here as quickly as you can. She writes a neat hand. Hurry up.'

'You're wanted,' said Tomsk, his golf clubs already over his shoulder, as he put his head round the Playroom door.

Shansi, who was sitting at a table in the corner with some plastic cups, little dishes of paints and some brushes in front of her, said, 'Please who wants Shansi, where?'

'Tobermory. Workshop. Quick,' said Tomsk and was gone.

Shansi neatly put her things away and went.

An hour later, Alderney, quite bursting with curiosity, was called for again on the inter-burrow-phone and asked to bring four snack lunches to the Workshop.

'What is going on I ask myself,' muttered Madame Cholet. 'Why can't they eat like other decent Wombles at the correct time at the correct place. What do they think this burrow is, a hotel?'

Alderney thought it best not to answer and Madame Cholet continued to grumble as she dished up four absolutely delicious helpings of dandelion and bark pie (with a touch of moss garlic) followed by oak-apple jelly with daisy cream. It was just as well she didn't see how this tasty meal was eaten, because for once the four Wombles concerned were actually thinking of work more than they were of food. All the food went, of course, but it was eaten in gulps, with forks and spoons being waved around as they all, or at least three of them, talked with their mouths full. Madame Cholet would have been horrified,

69

but luckily she was busy dishing out lunch for all the other Wombles, so she never had a moment to look round the Workshop door at what was going on.

A great deal was going on too. There were papers everywhere and bits of cardboard were pinned up on the shelves and being drawn over. In fact, paper was being used up at a rate which would have really distressed Miss Adelaide. But fortunately *she* was clearing up the Womblegarten and getting it ready for the afternoon's paw-craft lesson, and so was much too busy to put her head round the door.

In one corner Shansi, with her little pink tongue stuck out of one corner of her mouth, was writing in a notebook as fast as she could go. *Flip, flip, flip* went the pages as Tobermory told her what to write. She was too busy to wonder what was going on until later in the afternoon when Tobermory gave her quite a different sort of job to do.

And part of the result of all this activity was that just before supper time two beautifully written notices were pinned up on the corridor side of the Workshop door. The first one was headed:

SPECIAL PROJECT:
UNDERWATER FARMING:
ALL THOSE WOMBLES INTERESTED IN JOINING THIS PROJECT SHOULD SEE COUSIN BOTANY AT 8 P.M. IN THE PLAYROOM THIS EVENING.

And the second one was headed:

EMERGENCY!
SPECIAL AND EXTRA WOMBLE TIDY GROUPS NEEDED.

70

ALL THOSE INTERESTED IN *SPECIAL DUTIES* SHOULD
SEE *TOBERMORY* AT 8 P.M. IN THE WORKSHOP
THIS EVENING.

'There,' said Tobermory. 'That should get the ball rolling, I think.'

CHAPTER 8

MISS ADELAIDE PUTS HER FOOT DOWN

The burrow was soon absolutely buzzing with activity, with Wombles scurrying about in all directions. Tobermory had been quite right, twice over. The ball was definitely rolling and all the quarrelling and fighting had stopped as if by magic. Of course, Orinoco volunteered to help Cousin Botany, and he was so relieved that he wasn't going to be half starved that he was almost embarrassingly grateful.

'Oh, all right, all right,' said Botany, swiping at the beaming Orinoco with his awful hat, 'no need to go on so. We're not out of the wood yet. First off we've got to start tunnelling . . .'

'Tunnelling!'

' 'Sright. Tobermory's worked out the lay of the land round the burrow so that we can see which way the water flows when it rains. They're called cul-something or other, but to me they're little valleys and so I shall call 'em. Now what we has to do is to work out which little valleys we pipes the water from back to here. See?'

'Sort of. Do you mean there'll be digging work?'

'Ah.'

'I'm not very strong, you know,' said Orinoco, backing towards the door. 'In fact, I'm really rather a delicate sort of Womble and . . .'

'Nothing like a bit of digging to make you strong then,' said Botany. 'Collect your spade at six o'clock sharp!'

'Oh dear,' mumbled Orinoco. 'No sooner is one difficulty all nicely finished with when along comes another. I think I'll have a double helping of breakfast to get my strength up.'

Alderney too had asked to work on underwater farming and to her surprise found this meant that she had to help Madame Cholet clear out the larders, so as to find new containers for all these exciting foods which would soon, they hoped, be coming into the burrow.

'*Alors,*' said Madame Cholet. 'We have so few nice little jars and plastic boxes left. The Human Beings don't throw them away like they used to,' and she almost sighed for the Bad Old Days when there had been almost too much dumped rubbish for the Wombles to tidy away and make use of again.

'They still dump bottles,' said Alderney, who was swishing away with a mop in a bowl of soapy water. 'I mean lemonade bottles and milk bottles and things like that. And tins . . .'

'True, my little one, true. Gently, please, you are washing the jars not the floor. Tobermory has asked for every tin that is tidied to be sent straight

73

to the Workshop. He says it is because of the Emergency. He says.' And Madame Cholet gave a loud sniff to show what she thought of this idea.

'Couldn't we use lemonade bottles?' asked Alderney.

'Of course, we do so. For bracken juice, dandelion cough mixture, fizzy buttercup and so on and so on. But also one needs the jars for dried this and that and so forth. It is very difficult for a cook, especially a good cook, to have to work without the proper equipment! Now when I was young . . .'

And off went Madame Cholet but, as she was quite interesting to listen to, Alderney didn't mind too much. Also she wanted to learn to be a good cook herself one day, so she was keen to pick up any tips that were going.

The young Wombles were let off work at dusk and met for a few rounds of 'Great Uncle Bulgaria's Footsteps' which is a very skilful, rather scary game that Tomsk won easily.

'Let's have some more,' he suggested.

'No fear, I'm far too tired,' said Orinoco, who had anyway sat out, or rather dozed out, the last few rounds. 'I've had an *awful* day. Nothing but work. I'm *exhausted*.'

'I bet your day wasn't as bad as mine . . .'

'Or mine . . .'

'Or mine . . .'

'Me too,' echoed Shansi.

'*You're* all right,' grumbled Orinoco, 'all you do is writing. Anyone can write. That's not work. I dare say I could write a whole book if I wanted to. A jolly good book it'd be too.'

'Am not writing book,' said Shansi. 'Am writing

out many notes for Tobermory. Am using much paper too.'

She sounded a bit worried and Wellington, who had been sitting thinking about his beautiful and apparently useless oil rig, said kindly, 'It's not your fault. Those men Terry and John said there was a worldwide shortage of paper, but it's not your fault.'

Which well-meant remark made Shansi feel more guilty than ever.

'I bet I worked harder than anybody,' said Alderney, and she told them about cleaning out the larders and storerooms and how they were running out of jars and how Tobermory was taking all the tins.

'I picked up enough lemonade bottles today,' said Wellington, who with Tomsk was working for the Special Duties Section. 'Of course, they'd be the wrong shape, but if you got rid of the long neck part . . . oh, hold on.' And he put his hands over his ears and screwed his eyes tightly shut. Everybody kept a respectful silence as they knew that these were the signs that Wellington was having one of his Ideas. Sometimes they worked too, although not always, as in the case of the oil rig.

'A grinder. Something to grind with,' muttered Wellington.

'Teeth?' suggested Orinoco, yawning and scratching. 'I can grind anything with my teeth . . .'

'Not bottles, you couldn't,' said Wellington. 'See you later. Excuse me,' and he went trotting back to the burrow where he burst into the Workshop, skipped round Tobermory and vanished into the back storeroom where he could be heard muttering. 'Something very hard. A metal blade. A clamp. A wheel. And sandpaper. Must have sandpaper.'

'Now what's he up to,' Tobermory said aloud, but he couldn't hear his own words as he had a lot of welding to do which is a fairly noisy occupation if you are right on top of it. Sparks went shooting in all directions, but not, of course, into Tobermory's eyes as he was wearing goggles which were attached to his bowler hat and gave him a fearsome expression.

Probably the truth was that Tobermory had been working harder than anyone, for ever since the notice had been put up on the Workshop door and the two meetings had been held, a new spirit had pervaded the burrow. Everybody had begun to work so hard that Tobermory had been showered with old tin cans of every size and shape. His working party had sorted them, scoured them and removed their lids and bottoms with Tobermory's patent lid-remover, which left no raw edges. The working party had also painted the tins—and quite a bit of themselves—both inside and out with Tobermory's patent preservative-and-anti-rust paint, but it had been left to the old grey Womble to do the laborious job of welding all these treated tins into the pipelines which would be needed for the underwater farming scheme.

Tobermory welded the umpteenth tin of the last eight hours and turned down his blowtorch and lifted up his goggles. The muttering was still going on in the back storeroom, interspersed with little grunts and thumps and once by 'Ouch, ouch, ouch, that was my finger. Ouch'.

'You all right?' asked Tobermory, who felt too tired to get down off his carpenter's stool.

'Yes, thank you. I'm inventing, you know.'

'I thought you might be. Can I ask what?'

There was a slight pause and then Wellington's face appeared round the door as he said apologetically, 'Would you mind awfully if I didn't say, please, Tobermory? Only it might not work like you-know-what and then you feel such a Womble twit.'

'Suit yourself,' said Tobermory. 'Only be careful, do.'

And Tobermory pulled his mask down and prepared to tackle the umpteenth-and-one tin of the day. He was so intent on what he was doing that he never noticed that Wellington left the Workshop with a handkerchief round one paw, a smile right across his face and with his latest invention under one arm.

Although he was very excited and longing to show Madame Cholet his present for her, Wellington slept without moving all night as did all the other Wombles. Not even the chill draught which whistled through the gap under the front door could keep one of them awake, and when Tobermory finally got to his bed he started to snore the moment he got his head on the pillow.

Everybody overslept and there just wasn't time to get along to the kitchen before Wellington had to go off on tidying-up work, and as there had been a high wind in the night, all kinds of rubbish had landed on the Common.

'It jolly well *would*,' muttered Wellington, tying his long scarf over the top of his cap to keep it on. 'Just when we don't want any litter, we get tons of it. Whoops!'

It *was* whoops too, for the wind nearly blew him

over and he had to hang on to a sapling. Tomsk, who was ahead of Wellington, got caught unawares as he was halfway across an open patch of ground and the next thing he knew he was being bowled along with his tidy-bag ballooning out like a sail ahead of him.

'Yip, wow, help,' bellowed Tomsk, hanging on grimly to his bag as no Womble ever lets go of anything except under extreme pressure. But there was nobody about to help him and like a large grey furry ball Tomsk went bounding across the Common, now on his stomach, then on his seat as the gale-force wind took charge of him. He was practically out of sight by the time he finally managed to make a grab for a tree and he was going so fast that he careered twice round the tree before he sank to the ground feeling quite breathless.

'Well,' said Tomsk, 'well, I never. Hallo, what's happened there!'

He was close to the edge of the road and, although it was very early in the morning, a group of Human Beings were standing staring at something. So, of course, Tomsk had to go and stare too, and he crept forward through some bushes on his hands and knees until he managed to see that a large lorry was lying on its side. It was one of those lorries that have no sides to them and it didn't take Tomsk more than a minute to work out what must have happened. The lorry had obviously been piled high with large flat pieces of plastic, for they were now scattered far and wide. Like Tomsk, the lorry must have been suddenly caught by a powerful gust of wind and with its high load it had just been blown over. The driver didn't seem to be hurt, just annoyed as he told all the people exactly why it wasn't his fault. The people all seemed to agree with him and then they all turned and looked down the road as a breakdown van came into view and drew up ahead of the lorry.

It was really quite interesting watching how the men got the lorry back on its feet again so to speak, with a thuddering jar which made it bounce a bit. Then some of the men picked up the unbroken pieces of plastic and shoved them back on to the lorry, but the pieces which had got chipped they just pushed into the bushes.

'Leave 'em,' said the driver. 'There's no point in taking that lot back to the factory. Thanks, mates . . .'

And five minutes later the lorry and the van with the crane on its back had gone and so had all the people. What was left was Tomsk and a number of sheets of plastic. Tomsk eyed it doubtfully. It would have to be tidied up, of course, but how? He was still considering this question slowly and carefully when Wellington, his tidy-bag folded under his arm, joined him.

'No good trying to tidy up in this wind,' puffed Wellington. 'We'll have to wait till it drops. It keeps *on* coming and going. It doesn't seem to be able to make up its mind *what* to do, drat it. How did all this plastic stuff get here, I wonder? I should've thought it was too heavy to have been blown.'

'Well, it was sort of blown,' said Tomsk and slowly explained.

'I see,' said Wellington at the finish. 'You'd better go back to the burrow and get some transport and a good strong rope. I'll keep watch here.'

'All right,' agreed Tomsk and he'd gone quite a long way before it occurred to him that he ought to have asked what Wellington meant by 'transport'. He tried to explain his dilemma to Tobermory who was now surrounded by lengths of pipe and hard at work again with his noisy blow-torch.

'You're not having WOM 1,' growled Tobermory. 'I don't want it getting all scratched. You'll have to take the wheelbarrow. The rope's on the shelf marked ROPE. Now stop bothering me, do.'

It took Tomsk and Wellington the best part of two hours to get the wheelbarrow properly stacked up and its load secured, let alone back to the burrow. Luckily the wind had died down for the moment, but the barrow was so heavily loaded that it kept swerving first one way and then another, and a couple of times it turned right round before they could stop it.

'What have you got there?' asked Orinoco, who had just tiptoed out of the burrow to wait for the trolley to come round. He'd had a double helping of breakfast all right, but the odd thing was that he felt hungrier than ever.

'It's a load of plastic sheeting which . . .'

'. . . fell off the back of a lorry,' put in Tomsk.

'Jolly good,' said Orinoco. 'Jolly clever too. Just what's needed. Hallo, I do believe the trolley's coming at last. I'm *starving*.'

'Needed?' queried Wellington cautiously.

'Um. Make a smashing front door with one of those plastic bits,' said Orinoco. 'That's what you brought it back for, isn't it? I wonder if I could manage *three* grass buns with daisy cream? Yes, I dare say I could.'

'Ah,' said Wellington slowly, 'yes, yes, of course. It will make a very good front door.' He heaved one of his enormous sighs. He was supposed to be the brainy one who had all the good ideas, and yet both Tomsk and Orinoco had come up with really smashing ones which he hadn't even thought of. It was funny how once somebody else thought of an idea it always seemed obvious.

Wellington sighed again and began to trundle the barrow into the burrow and then he remembered his own (if small) invention and brightened up. He parked the barrow neatly and darted down to get his surprise out of the box where he kept all his special treasures. He was halfway to the kitchen and just passing the Workshop when a voice which made prickles run up and down his fur stopped him dead in his tracks.

'Wellington,' said Miss Adelaide, appearing in the doorway of the Workshop, her toe tapping, 'as Tobermory appears to be elsewhere at the moment, perhaps *you* will be kind enough to explain!'

'Yes, Miss Adelaide,' said Wellington, although he hadn't the least idea what she was talking about. But Miss Adelaide (like Great Uncle Bulgaria) was not the kind of Womble that a young working Womble would question, except in very unusual circumstances. However, the moment he was inside the Workshop Wellington put two and two together with the speed of light.

'Oh!' he said and swallowed.

'Oh, it is indeed,' agreed Miss Adelaide, her toe tapping faster than ever. 'I thought I recognised your writing, Wellington! Together with the

81

writing of others, I must agree. Have you any notion just how much of our valuable paper you must have used up with your silly scribbling? Paper which is badly needed in the Womblegarten for the young ones? Hm?'

Wellington shook his head and Tobermory, coming into the Workshop and realising what was happening, looked, at that moment in spite of his advanced age, just as young and guilty as Wellington.

'I'm waiting for an explanation,' said Miss Adelaide. 'From both of you!'

'*Tsk, tsk, tsk*,' said Tobermory.

CHAPTER 9

THE BIG SPLASH

It took quite a long time to explain matters to Miss Adelaide and, even when this had been done, she still only sniffed and looked disapproving as she smoothed down her neat apron with silky grey paws.

'I see,' she said in exactly the tone of voice which meant that what she saw was how very silly and wasteful they had been, using up all that paper when it was so badly needed in the Womblegarten. She walked out at last with her nose very much in the air, and Tobermory and Wellington glanced at each other and let out two enormous sighs of relief.

'We'll have to do something about the dratted paper shortage,' said Tobermory, 'but what it is I haven't the faintest notion. You'd better have one of your Ideas, young Wellington.'

'I haven't had any at all lately,' said Wellington,

83

with his mouth turned right down at the corners. 'Everybody else seems to be having them instead.'

'Oh yes,' said Tobermory, hoisting himself on to his carpenter's stool. 'What's that in your paw then, ho-hum?'

'It's a surprise for Madame Cholet,' said Wellington.

'Well, off you nip and show it to her then,' ordered Tobermory and slid the welding mask down over his eyes as he reached for yet another tin tube.

Madame Cholet was at the kitchen table chopping up grass with the brisk *tick-tock-tick-tock* of an expertly held knife. Alderney was writing out labels for jars (what there were of them) and altogether the kitchen was a particularly nice, warm and friendly place for a young Womble who hadn't been very lucky recently.

Wellington put his surprise down on the kitchen table and Madame Cholet stopped chopping and put aside her knife and picked up Wellington's gift and went '*tsk, tsk, tsk*' several times. It was a nice little glass bottle with a tin lid which fitted snugly over the top.

'But how,' said Madame Cholet, 'how did you make it? And from what? Eh?'

'It's an old lemonade bottle that some Human Being chucked away. I sawed off the neck with a glass cutter I made, and smoothed the cut bit quite smooth with sandpaper and I made the lid thing from one of the tin lids that Tobermory doesn't want. Do you like it?'

'It is . . .' and Madame Cholet put her third finger and thumb together in a way which in France obviously meant 'superb'. 'How many such jars can you make, little Wellington? I can use dozens and dozens of them! Come, you shall have a special hot drink. You deserve it!'

'You *are* clever, Wellington,' said Alderney.

So what with this and that in no time at all Wellington felt a great deal better. Quite obviously his luck was in too, for soon after this a whole batch of milk bottles was brought in by a tidying-up party, and Wellington had to get a somewhat unwilling Orinoco to help him grind them down.

'I'll tell you what,' said Orinoco, 'there's far too much to do these days. I shall be glad when old Bungo gets back to lend a paw. He's a bossy sort of Womble, but one does miss him after a bit. Ouch, that was my finger, ouch, ouch, ouch . . .'

'You do have to be careful,' agreed Wellington, wiping his spectacles as they had misted up. 'Perhaps that grinder ought to have some kind of safety guard on it. How's the digging getting on? I agree about Bungo. Funny really.'

'What—the digging?' asked Orinoco somewhat indistinctly as he was sucking his bruised finger.

'No, how you can miss a Womble. I missed Great Uncle Bulgaria right away, but I did think it'd be quite good without old Bungo bossing one about. Still, he'd be an extra paw round the burrow now all right. How's the digging, Orinoco?'

'Very boring. You've seen one pipeline, you've seen 'em all. I wouldn't do it if I wasn't thinking of the good of the burrow, you know.'

Wellington almost started to say, 'The good of your stomach you mean', but he managed to stop himself.

'Dig, dig, dig,' went on Orinoco in an aggrieved tone, as he turned the little handle that made

85

Wellington's glass-cutting blade go round with a satisfactory *zzzzzz* sound as yet another neck was cut from a bottle. 'I suppose it'll work, but I don't see it myself. Supposing the wind keeps on coming and going and we don't get enough rain and the whole Project's an awful old flop! All my hard work will be for nothing, you know. And I've lost a great deal of weight over it.'

'Have you?' said Wellington doubtfully for Orinoco looked as fat as ever to him.

''Course. Come on, young Wellington, give us another bottle. It's nearly time for a nice little snack to keep up our strength.'

Tobermory, too, wasn't completely sure that this very grandiose plan for underwater farming was going to work. For years and years he had been hoarding in one of his many storerooms some large and very ugly iron tanks which had the letters EWS painted on them. A whole row of them had been left on the edge of the Common and when people had started dumping rubbish in them, Tobermory had arranged for the tanks to be transported back to the burrow. He had performed this great task by having the tanks slid across the grass on rollers made of saplings. It had been a dreadfully heavy, tiring job, especially when the Wombles had had to manoeuvre the tanks in through the door which normally only WOM I used, but he had been sure in his own mind that one day the tanks would come in useful—and now they had!

What was more, while he was making up a simple water cleansing and aerating system he had suddenly realised what the letters EWS probably stood for—EMERGENCY WATER SUPPLY! It was the sort of joke that Tobermory enjoyed and he had actually gone 'HO-HO-HO, HEH-HEH-HEH, *TSK-TSK-TSK*' to himself for several minutes. It had been a much needed moment of light relief for Tobermory had a great deal on his mind these days. There were endless problems piling up and he began to realise more and more just how much Great Uncle Bulgaria had had on his shoulders all these years. Only Cousin Botany, once again his old familiar almost silent self, seemed quite certain about the outcome of the Project. He went trotting here, there and everywhere, waving a paw at first this working party of Wombles and then at that one. The big tanks were now in position in the far end of the burrow. The lighting had already been connected and the pipelines were laid, except for the last few inches where they stopped just below the surface of the Common. The gale-force wind was still blowing, but Tobermory knew that the moment it dropped, the big rain clouds would come billowing in all ready to let loose their great burdens.

It was a nerve-racking period and all the Wombles felt it, even as they went about their double duties. Knowing how much it meant not only to Tobermory and Cousin Botany, but to all of them and the future which lay ahead, they crossed their paws behind their backs and waited.

'Zero Hour', which is what Tobermory had called it on the notice on the Workshop door, arrived with surprising suddenness, just as the last few inches of pipeline were finished and the 'plugs' inserted in them. These plugs were a really clever touch by Tobermory as they were made of wood and were covered with plastic grass, painted by

87

Shansi with here and there a daisy or a buttercup or a dandelion (also plastic) so that they merged into the Common.

The gale-force wind died as quickly as it had blown up and, sure enough, within two hours the rain started. The burrow was alerted instantly.

'All Wombles to their stations, all Wombles to their stations,' said Tobermory, who had himself been woken a mere three minutes earlier by the Nightwatch Womble, who happened to be Tomsk.

Everybody hurried to their own particular place, quite forgetting how tired and deep in sleep they had been only such a short while ago. Their eyes were bright and their fur was lying not quite flat which is a sure sign with a Womble that exciting things are happening. And of all of them Cousin Botany was probably the most excited, only he showed it the least as he pulled his awful hat firmly down on his head and marched into the first tank room. The Outside Womble Action Party scampered out of the burrow and made for their own particular places and then, ears at the alert, they heard Tobermory's whistle and up and down the Common as the rain began to *plop, plop* down on the grass, the ends of the pipelines were opened up and various small Wombles settled back, nicely protected from the rain by their thick fur, to wait for another blast on the whistle which would tell them to close the pipelines.

Down below, Tobermory paced up and down, his paws behind his back. But Cousin Botany stood placidly in the big tank room and waited. He didn't have to do so for long. First there was a *drip, drip, drip* and then a soft *shhhhhh* and a thin trickle of water came sliding down into the big tank. The

trickle grew thicker until it was quite a respectable stream which was gurgling into the tank from the pipes. Tobermory stared at the lapping water as if he could hardly believe it was really there and then, as the level grew higher and higher at a quite remarkable speed, he had to rush off and get the next lot of rainwater diverted into the next tank and then the next and the next. And all the pipes he had made so carefully not only held firm, but didn't leak a single drop.

It rained throughout the night and by the time a very pale sun struggled up over the edge of the Common there were some extremely wet Wombles still at work, closing down the pipe-lines, as the tanks down in the burrow were full of softly lapping water.

'Well,' said Cousin Botany, 'that's all right then. Thanks to you, Cousin Tobermory. Well done, old friend.'

They shook hands.

Tobermory slept in the next day and it was Cousin Botany who took charge of the following part of the proceedings. It was he who got his Womble Working Party on to moving his precious underwater plants from Queen's Mere to the burrow and quite a proceeding it was too.

They did try using Wellington's oil rig, but it wasn't precise enough as it kept bringing up rather smelly mud, a great many bubbles and all kinds of old rubbish as well as the plants. So quite early on Cousin Botany told Tomsk that he, Tomsk, had better dive down with a shovel and carefully bring up the precious plants. They were funny-looking things too, varying in colour from pale green to a deep emerald and from what looked like long stems of grass to fat little curly leaves.

Orinoco tried eating one of these as he carried a trayful of them back to the burrow, and his spirits fell considerably. The leaves had a bitter taste which made him screw up his mouth as though he had been sucking a lemon.

'I don't think I'm going to fancy this new food at all,' he muttered and he felt so mournful he had to go along to the kitchen to have a nice, sweet, daisy syrup day-cap.

'Never mind,' said Alderney. 'Have it in one of our new mugs. Aren't they pretty?'

They were too. For Alderney handed the drink over to Orinoco in a good sensible mug with lovely blue pictures on it.

'Who tidied that up?' asked Orinoco.

'Nobody. Miss Adelaide and I made them,' said Alderney, stopping her usual headlong rush, so that she could admire her own work. 'There was all that old paper Tobermory and Cousin Botany and

Wellington had drawn their maps and diagrams on, and it seemed a pity to waste it completely, so we scrunched it all up and soaked it in water and when it got nice and soft we made it into all kinds of things which we varnished. Mugs, plates, bowls, jugs, dishes. Miss Adelaide's got all the Womblegarten making things now.'

'But what about the painting on the outside?' asked Orinoco. 'When I was in the Womblegarten we made things out of paper and water too, but they never looked like this!'

'That's Shansi,' said Alderney. 'She's ever so good at painting. She calls it Womble Willow Pattern. Isn't that nice?'

'It's not bad,' agreed Orinoco, squinting at the picture which showed three fat little Wombles crossing a bridge carrying their tidy-bags while a couple of pigeons flew overhead.

'Shansi started painting on old plastic cups that were tidied up on the Common, but they don't last. They split and crack. The things that the Womblegarten are making will go on for ages, unless they're dropped. And I'll tell you what,' Alderney lowered her voice and beckoned to Orinoco. 'Miss Adelaide's not nearly as cross as she was, now that the Womblegarten's working so well. But she does need unused paper for sums and writing and stuff like that. So if you see any, don't forget. Another daisy syrup?'

'OK, I'll remember. Thanks, don't mind if I do.'

It was a great deal of hard work to transfer all Botany's underwater farm and by the finish everybody was exhausted, although very pleased with themselves as they went from tank to tank looking at these strange plants. Not everybody was

91

sure that they were going to fancy this new food but, as the Wombles are the most polite creatures in the whole world, nobody quite liked to say so.

'*Tiens*,' said Madame Cholet, who had had a taste or two herself and who like Orinoco had found the plants rather bitter. 'I shall have to think of some new recipes. This is how a real cook should be! Ready to welcome a challenge, and as I am a very good cook indeed I shall overcome this trifling difficulty. Ah yes, a little clover honey perhaps and a touch of bark syrup and then maybe a *soupçon* of dandelion oil . . .'

Madame Cholet rolled up her sleeves, got out a bowl or two, some spoons, a measuring jug, a couple of saucepans and got down to work. She mixed, tasted, rolled things round her tongue, rinsed out her mouth, adjusted this and that and then began to smile as she said to herself, 'Ah yes, of course . . . now then, mixed with a little grass flour and kneaded out flat and fried carefully, that would be most tasteful. What should I call it? Ah, of course . . . *quel dommage!*'

'Well, that's that then,' said Cousin Botany, taking off his awful old hat and wiping round the inside of it with a corner of his apron. 'Thanks very much, all. Hallo then, who's that?'

'It's me,' said Wellington, emerging out of the shadows with his oil rig and bucket on the faithful wheelbarrow. He knew the rig was a failure, but somehow he couldn't quite bear to part with it. It had seemed such a *very* good idea at the time.

'That bucket doesn't half smell, young Wellington,' said Botany. 'What you got in it, eh?'

'Just bits of the bottom of Queen's Mere,' replied Wellington who was tired and cold and dispirited. Inventing a new way of using old throwaway glass bottles is not the same as discovering how to drill for oil.

'It does pong,' agreed Tomsk, holding his nose. 'I should leave it there if I was you. 'Night all.'

And off went Tomsk, shaking the last of the Queen's Mere water out of his thick fur as he made for the burrow and bed. Cousin Botany gave Wellington a pat on the back and then returned to his underwater farming tanks. He still couldn't quite believe that they really existed and that all his work of years and years had at last been proved useful.

Wellington heaved one of his great big sighs and then jumped as a gentle voice said from the shadows, 'What is in bucket, please?'

'Dredgings from Queen's Mere.'

'Oh yes.'

Shansi edged forward and looked into the bucket, wrinkling up her nose.

'I know it pongs,' said Wellington crossly.

'Not smell which makes me stop. Is what is made of and colour of same. Most interesting.'

'Now look here,' said Wellington, sitting up with a jerk. He had begun to nod off. 'If *you're* going to have an Idea, please don't. Wombles have had Ideas all round me recently and . . .'

Shansi didn't say anything, but just handed the bucket over to him. Wellington took it and sniffed and then looked and finally put one finger into it. The finger came out very black indeed.

Wellington looked at Shansi and then back at the bucket.

'Oh, my word,' said Wellington and he licked his finger, rubbed his spectacles, screwed up his eyes and sniffed. 'Hold on,' he said. 'I think I *am* having another Idea. Oh dear, dear, dear ME!'

CHAPTER 10

ORINOCO ON TELEVISION

Everything now began to happen so quickly that none of the Wombles seemed to have time to draw breath, let alone quarrel or fight among themselves. Even the arrival of Great Uncle Bulgaria's next letter was, although interesting, no more than a nice thirty minutes in which to have a sit down while sipping a refreshing bracken juice.

Orinoco, recuperating from all his pipeline digging, was only too glad to go and help Madame Cholet in the kitchen and to taste, mix, add and generally give his advice. Alderney was kept at full stretch filling and labelling all the new jars which Wellington had made with Orinoco's help. Cousin Botany was forever going round and round his precious under-Common tanks, making sure that his plants were getting enough fresh water and light. He had even begun to feed them some compost from the pile he had started beneath the undergrowth by the Mere.

Tobermory, having had a good rest, was now working on adapting the tidied-up plastic sheets. The brace and bit which he had repaired earlier was coming in useful as the plastic was very hard indeed.

'It'll never wear out or get woodworm, that's for certain,' said Tobermory, who was wearing his goggles again. 'The only difficulty is, it won't look the same as the old door.'

'Ah,' said Shansi, a wicked gleam in her round little eyes as she bowed politely. 'Can promise it will!'

'All right, cleversticks,' growled Tobermory, 'just hold that side still, while I saw this one. Plastic is all very well in its way, but it's not the same as wood, say what you like!'

'We see,' said Shansi with a slight giggle.

Meanwhile Wellington had set up his own particular tests at the back of the Workshop. Tests which included a bucketful of the bottom of Queen's Mere. The smell was so awful that he had to tie his scarf across his mouth, but he was quite determined to carry on with what he was doing, because it might at last make his ex-oil rig become useful.

And it was some days later that Wellington slid off his workbench stool holding up two glassfuls of liquid. He gazed at them and nodded happily. The glass in his left paw was full of a thick yellow liquid, while the glass in his right paw was blacker than the night when there is no moon.

'Now,' said Wellington, 'all I need are a couple of felt tips and I'll show 'em all!'

By 'them' Wellington meant Miss Adelaide

and Tobermory, and although both these older Wombles happened to be very busy discussing some important news in the Workshop, they knew at once that Wellington's polite invitation to see his invention must be accepted instantly.

'Back so soon. And a good thing too,' growled Tobermory, putting down the letter he had been reading.

'Which must mean that the whole business has been a great success,' said Miss Adelaide. 'One hopes.'

'Taste this, please,' said Madame Cholet, bustling in from the kitchen. 'I have put just a touch of my new paste on these grass biscuits. *C'est* OK?'

'Um. Rather,' agreed Tobermory, crunching up his biscuit and then licking his lips while wiping the back of his paw along his grey moustache. 'Smashing. Have you read Bulgaria's letter?'

'Oh yes, Adelaide passed it to me yesterday. I think, Tobermory, that for you in particular it will be good to have Bulgaria back home. You have lost weight, and for a Womble to do that is very bad. It reflects, you see, on my cooking!'

'*Tsk, tsk, tsk*,' said Tobermory, taking off his bowler hat and running a handkerchief round the inside of it. 'Never, never. Ho-hum. It's young Wellington that we must think of now. He hasn't invented all that he felt he should have done, but he does come up with some very good ideas from time to time and now I believe he's done it again. All right, young Wellington, in you come.'

Wellington edged into the Workshop rather shyly and then, reassured by the smiles and nods of the older Wombles, he produced two flasks from

97

behind his back. In one flask was a thick yellow liquid while in the other the liquid was blacker than the blackest night.

Wellington bowed jerkily and said, 'I think I've discovered an oil, sort of, which will stop all the doors making horrible noises when they're opened and shut. I discovered it quite by accident. This is it.' And he held up the flask which was yellow-coloured.

'What's in it?' asked Tobermory.

'I'm not too sure really,' said Wellington. 'It's some buttercup juice mixed with part of the stuff which came up with my ex-oil rig. But it is *ever* so oily.'

And Wellington tipped the flask slightly so that a few drops of yellow liquid slowly fell, *glup, glup, glup*, on to the table.

'And what is in the other bottle?' enquired Miss Adelaide, as Tobermory put one cautious finger into the mixture and first sniffed and then tasted it.

'Ink. Or paint,' said Wellington. 'Honestly, Miss Adelaide, it's *ever* so black, and you dip a felt tip into it and then draw on a plastic blackboard. Look, Shansi will show you . . .'

Wellington stood aside and Shansi came into the Workshop, ducking her head rather shyly. In her hands she held a pile of small sheets of coloured plastic. She sat down at the workbench and, taking a felt-tipped paintbrush out of her pocket, she dipped it into the flask which held the black liquid, pressed it gently against the side to get rid of the excess and then, with what looked like half a dozen quick strokes, she painted the Womble Willow Pattern on a piece of scarlet plastic.

'Very good,' said Miss Adelaide, 'very good

indeed, dear. But then you always were top of the painting class. This really could be hung on the wall as a picture. We do miss your skills in the Womblegarten, Shansi. Indeed I have been wondering if . . .'

'But, Miss Adelaide,' burst out Wellington, who could stand the suspense no longer, 'it's not a picture. It's a new kind of slate which you use in the Womblegarten instead of paper exercise books. You can wipe off the drawing or the writing or whatever it is frightfully easily with a cloth. Then you have a clean slate again. Do you like it? Do you think it's a good Idea?'

Young Wombles, even young working Wombles, hardly ever interrupt Miss Adelaide and get away without a telling-off or a cuff round the ear. Sometimes they get both. But even as Wellington realised what he had done and began to gulp nervously, Miss Adelaide nodded and smiled.

'Yes, it is a good Idea,' she agreed. 'Helpful, practical and *simple* . . .'

This was said with a sideways glance at Tobermory, who pretended to be busy trying to re-mend the brace and bit, which had started giving trouble again after having to deal with heavy duty plastic. He knew jolly well that Miss Adelaide didn't altogether approve of the underwater farming scheme. But then she was rather set in her ways and anything that was as new as that would be sure to take her a while to get used to.

'These boards and pens will also solve the chalk shortage,' Miss Adelaide went on. 'I should like a big board for my own use when I am teaching. Congratulations, Wellington. Now, as I was saying before I was—ahem—interrupted, I think it would be a good idea if Shansi stopped doing tidying-up work and returned to help me in the Womblegarten.'

'Am not clever,' said Shansi.

'Yes, you are. You're very good at making things and painting and decorating. I shall put you in charge of the paw-craft class.'

Shansi thought this over for all of five seconds and then nodded violently.

'Would like,' said Shansi, 'would like VERY much.'

'Some Wombles have all the luck,' said Orinoco, when he heard this latest piece of news. 'Now that's just the kind of job I ought to have really. I'm quite a good artist, you know.'

'No, I didn't,' said Wellington truthfully.

'Oh yes, I can draw terribly good pin-Wombles and . . .' Orinoco stopped suddenly and then went on quickly, 'Well, I'd better nip off and finish my tidying-up. See you later.'

'I thought you'd finished for today,' said Wellington, but he spoke to the empty air for Orinoco, moving at a fair speed, was already yards away and heading for the open Common. His strange behaviour was explained almost instantly, for at that moment Tobermory and Tomsk came into view carrying between them, and with much groaning and grunting, a large piece of brown plastic.

'New front door,' puffed Tobermory. 'Don't just stand there, young Wellington, come and lend us a paw. You need to build up your muscles or you'll get as fat as Orinoco. Funny, I thought I saw him here a minute ago. We could have done with his help too.'

100

Wellington looked in the direction of his friend, who was now a mere round furry dot on the horizon. It was very odd about Orinoco—he sometimes took a lot more exercise avoiding work than the actual work would have needed.

However, once he was well clear of the burrow, Orinoco slowed to a walk and then a saunter while he kept a weather eye open for somewhere to have a nice forty winks. There was what looked like a promising little line of trees over there with some nice cosy bushes growing round them, and beyond there was an old green van, which would make a good windbreak.

From his tidy-bag, Orinoco shook out the coat he'd picked up from the storeroom, for the wind was still a bit nippy, and put it on. It trailed round his feet, but that made it even cosier and, tying his hat on with his scarf, Orinoco slid a pair of dark glasses on to his nose, a toffee into his mouth and prepared to snuggle down in the bracken.

'Excuse me,' said a somewhat irritable voice, 'but you are knocking against our microphone, sir.'

Orinoco, not a Womble to get flustered, turned round and saw a largish man wearing headphones, coming out of the bushes on all fours.

'Sorry,' said Orinoco, and couldn't resist asking, 'What is the microphone *for*?'

'We're from WTV,' the man said importantly. 'We're doing a TV programme on the wildlife of Wimbledon Common.'

'Wild?' said Orinoco, faintly surprised. 'I didn't know there was much *wild* life, it always seems fairly tame to me. The squirrels tear about a bit sometimes in the spring, but they're not exactly *wild*. Silly sort of animals really, you can never get a sensible word out of 'em.'

The man stared very hard at Orinoco, who hitched up his trailing skirts, shunted the toffee to the other side of his mouth and prepared to move on. Great Uncle Bulgaria had always told his Wombles not to get involved with Human Beings if it was possible.

'Are you—are you a naturalist?' the man asked.

'No, I don't think so. I'm too busy for hobbies and games and things. I've had to find all sorts of ways round this silly old shortage business, you know.'

A shorter, dark-haired man had now appeared holding an unusual-looking camera on his shoulder. Orinoco wasn't too keen on having his photograph taken, but at the same time he couldn't resist showing off a little. Nobody back at the burrow had been listening to him much recently, and it was rather pleasant having an audience, even if they were only Human Beings.

'What sort of shortages?' the larger man asked.

'Food,' said Orinoco in an offhand voice. 'I mean, it's obvious that to stop us running out of it we have to grow more stuff underwater. There's plenty of water about still. And then you can use plastic instead of wood for all kinds of things like doors and shelves and drawing boards. You can produce oil out of deep sludge if you add crushed buttercups. Then, of course, old lemonade bottles properly ground down make jolly good jars and old newspapers are easy to turn into plates and cups and so on . . .'

Orinoco became aware that both the men were continuing to stare at him in an unblinking silence which made him start to feel nervous.

102

'Well, well,' said Orinoco, regretfully deciding that he'd better look for somewhere else to have his forty winks, 'I must be moving on.'

'Yes, yes, of course,' said the dark-haired man. 'It's been most interesting listening to you. Underwater farming—*of course!*'

'Sludge and buttercups?' said the other man, shaking his head. 'I wonder, could we have your name, sir?'

Orinoco, truthful as all Wombles are even in the most difficult situations, gave it, slightly indistinctly owing to the fact that the toffee had got stuck to his front teeth. He then bowed politely and trailed off through the bushes while the men watched him.

'What an extraordinary character,' said the larger man whose name was Terry. 'I'm sure I've seen him somewhere before. Perhaps on TV. What did he say his name was?'

'Orin Wandle,' said the dark-haired man whose name was John.

'Yes, I'm sure I've heard of him. I think he's a professor. Yes, yes, Professor Orin Wandle. He's one of the world's great experts on the Energy and Food Crisis. Surely *you've* heard of him?'

'Oh yes,' said Terry in an offhand way, 'yes, yes. *And* we've got him on film! We'll put him in the programme.'

Which is how Orinoco became the first Womble to appear on television and to give some sensible, down to earth advice on ways to deal with shortages of this and that. The older Wombles, when they heard about it, were very cross, but the younger members of the burrow thought it was marvellous and kept on asking him for his autograph. But Orinoco never got big-headed

103

about his sudden fame, because the name they made him sign was 'Orin Wandle'.

'Lot of nonsense,' grumbled Tobermory, who was in a bad temper, because the brace and bit had finally broken completely, which had made it very difficult for him to repair the shelves, the other doors and everything else. 'Thank goodness Great Uncle Bulgaria gets back tomorrow. He can't get here a moment too soon for me and that's a fact. *Tsk, tsk, tsk!*'

CHAPTER 11

REMEMBER YOU'RE A WOMBLE

'Well, it is pleasant to be home again,' said Great Uncle Bulgaria.

'Nice to have you back,' said Tobermory with such an enormous sigh of relief that his bowler hat lifted off his head. He took it off and wiped round the inside and replaced it. 'What was it like in America, Bulgaria?'

'Our American cousins were most hospitable,' said Great Uncle Bulgaria after the slightest pause, 'perhaps a little too much so occasionally. They can be somewhat overwhelming. But kind, extremely kind. Cousin Yellowstone sent you his warmest regards.'

'Kind of him.'

'Ho-hum,' agreed Great Uncle Bulgaria looking over the top of his spectacles, his little eyes twinkling. 'By the way, Tobermory, I brought you back a small present. Allow me to give it to you.'

It was a parcel which was surprisingly heavy for its size and as Tobermory neatly undid the wrappings he couldn't imagine what it could be. It was the most expensive kind of brace and bit. Not quite new of course, but in first-rate condition nevertheless.

'My word. Well. *Tsk, tsk, tsk,*' said Tobermory, brushing up his grey moustache with the back of his paw. 'Exactly what I wanted. Many, many thanks, Bulgaria. But how did you *know*?'

'I didn't. I just reasoned that you'd have a great deal of repair work to do and that your old what-yer-me-call was in a shaky condition so that you'd probably need a replacement. I got this one from Yellowstone's stores. Dear me, Tobermory, you've no idea of the *amount* of stuff that those American Wombles have got put away. Shelf after shelf, room after room. You'd find it fascinating!'

'Wimbledon's good enough for me,' said Tobermory. 'If I feel like a change I'll drive up to see the MacWomble the Terrible in Scotland. That's as far as I mean to go at my time of life. But what was the Conference like, Bulgaria?'

'Interesting. Constructive. I'll tell you all about it when we have our little party,' said Great Uncle Bulgaria a shade evasively. He added, 'The trip has done young Bungo good. Silly sort of name but it suits him. Knocked some of the bounce out of him. Those American Wombles were FAR bouncier. Ho, ho, ho. But tell me, Tobermory, what has been happening here?'

'After you've had a good day's rest,' said Tobermory. 'You're looking remarkably well, Bulgaria, but you've had a long journey. We'll tell you everything at the party. Sleep well, Bulgaria, old friend.'

The rest of the burrow was fairly humming with excitement for the next few hours, although all the Wombles were supposed to be resting. Somehow everything seemed completely safe and pleasant now that Great Uncle Bulgaria was home, added to which, of course, the burrow was now a great deal more comfortable than it had been when he left. Finally there was the picnic down by the Mere to look forward to.

At dusk all the Wombles lined up with their tidy-bags full, not of litter on this occasion, but delicious packets of food and cartons of drink. They were all nudging and pushing and whispering until Great Uncle Bulgaria came out of his study and then everybody cheered. They cheered so loudly that the sound reached Cousin Botany who, as usual, was working away with his beloved plants in the underwater farming rooms.

'Now what would that be for, I wonder?' said Cousin Botany, pushing back his awful old hat and scratching his chin.

He soon found out, because ten seconds later Tomsk put his head round the door and said in his rumbling voice, 'Come on, Cousin Botany, picnic time. You've got to be there, because,' and then Tomsk stopped suddenly and grinned. He took hold of Cousin Botany's arm and gently but firmly marched him off to join the others.

The moon was coming up and all the Wombles gathered round Great Uncle Bulgaria, who was sitting on a stool a little way up the bank. Tobermory and Madame Cholet came into view pushing the wheelbarrow, lodged inside which was a strange square object which was Tobermory's patent picnic stove. He pumped up the pressure and got it going and Madame Cholet placed a simply enormous frying pan on the top, and began to fry some little round, flat, green, biscuity-looking things. The smell was so delicious that everybody stopped talking (even Bungo who was rapidly becoming his old bossy self again) and just sniffed.

'Plates, plates, one at a time,' said Madame Cholet and on to each pretty blue and white newly made plate she slid one of these biscuity things.

'How tasty, how extremely tasty,' said Great Uncle Bulgaria when he had finished his down to the last and tiniest crumb. 'I've never had anything like it before. What is it?'

Madame Cholet waved her cooking slice at Cousin Botany, who still seemed to be in something of a dream.

'It is my latest culinary invention,' said Madame Cholet, 'and I wish to call it a "Botany Burger", as without *cher* Cousin Botany it could not have been made.'

Everybody clapped, even Cousin Botany, until he realised they were congratulating him, whereupon he seemed to become very interested in the faded ribbon which ran round his hat. Great Uncle Bulgaria looked thoughtful and ate the rest of his picnic without speaking. He was preparing himself for his speech. It was quite astonishingly short.

'Wombles of Wimbledon,' said Great Uncle Bulgaria, leaning on his stick and looking over the top of his spectacles at all their interested faces in the moonlight. 'Bungo and I have travelled a good many thousand miles during the last weeks. We

have met some of the oldest and wisest Wombles in the world, all of whom had gathered together to discuss the problem of world shortages of this and that. And what did we discover?'

Nobody moved, they just stared, wondering whatever was coming next. It sounded very, VERY serious.

'That every single solution these wise old Wombles put forward at the Conference had already been thought of. And what's more, put into practice!'

'Really?' said Tobermory.

'Good gracious me!' said Miss Adelaide.

'*Alors!*' said Madame Cholet.

Everybody else looked at his or her neighbour in wonderment.

'By whom, you may ask,' said Great Uncle Bulgaria, as nobody had asked. 'I'll tell you. By all of you. When you were all sleeping this afternoon I had a stroll round the entire burrow.'

'I might have known it,' Tobermory said under

109

his breath.

Great Uncle Bulgaria went on serenely.

'What did I find? I found a flourishing underwater farm. A farm which I now realise can produce such delicious delicacies as Botany Burgers! I found plastic being used in an entirely new way. I found . . . but you know all about it, because *you* were the ones who had all these ideas and put them into practice. Wombles of Wimbledon, I congratulate you and I'm proud of you and all your hard work.'

Everybody felt very proud of themselves and also rather shy and then Great Uncle Bulgaria clapped his white paws together and said briskly, 'And now let's have some music. Come along, young Wombles, you've sat still for long enough. Now you'd better take a bit of exercise.'

'I'll tell you what,' said Bungo as he and Orinoco, Alderney and Shansi, Wellington and Tomsk, lined up for a Womble barn dance, 'America's all right, but it's not half as good as Wimbledon Common. Of course it's *bigger*. I'll grant you *that*, but I'll tell you what . . .'

'No, you won't,' said Tomsk, picking his friend up by the scruff of his neck and turning him round. 'You'll shut up.'

'Oh, it's smashing being back,' said Bungo, grinning right across his face, and as usual taking absolutely no notice of what anybody else said. 'Are we ready then? A-one. A-two. A-three and away we go, altogether now!

'Remember you're a Womble, remember you're a Womble . . .'

WONDERFUL WOMBLING FACTS

 Wombles choose their names from places, cities and rivers found in Great Uncle Bulgaria's atlas of the world.

 Young Wombles spend their time in the Womblegarten, run by Miss Adelaide Womble, until they are old enough to tidy up outside.

 Midsummer's Eve is the most important night in the Wombles' year. They have a big party and eat far too much.

 There are Womble burrows all over the world, including Hyde Park in London, Loch Ness in Scotland, Yellowstone Park in the USA, and the Khyber Pass on the border of Pakistan and Afghanistan. The main burrow is underneath Wimbledon Common, South-west London.

 Fortune and Bason is Orinoco's favourite shop.

 Great Uncle Bulgaria's middle name is Coburg.